Snow Ordinary Family

Alaska Cozy Mystery
Book 10

Wendy Meadows

Chapter One

Sarah felt her feet begin to do a funny dance on the icy sidewalk in front of her coffee shop. "Oh no!" she cried and then slipped and sprawled flat on her backside on the ice.

"Los Angeles!" Amanda yelled, fighting back laughter. "Are you okay?"

Sarah slowly rubbed her back, eased up on one elbow, and looked up at Amanda's grinning face. "I'm fine, June Bug," she grumbled as heavy snow continued to fall down onto her face. Daylight was beginning to break, giving light to a powerful snow storm that showed no signs of stopping. "We should have stayed in Los Angeles with Pete."

Amanda carefully eased across the snow-covered sidewalk, gently treading on the hidden ice underneath, and leaned down to help her friend. "We helped Pete solve his case," she said in a proud voice. "It was time to come home."

"I know," Sarah replied, forcing a smile to her face. Sure, she had slipped and busted her backside. Sure, her clothes were coated in snow. Sure, she was frozen solid. But...well, life was good. "Help me stand up, June Bug."

Amanda took Sarah's gloved hand and helped the bruised woman get to her feet. "We'll open the café for a few hours and then go spend the rest of the day shopping at O'Mally's," she said over the icy winds. "And tonight, we'll eat at the diner. My treat."

"Deal," Sarah beamed. "We'll make it a girls-only week. Since our husbands are so rudely yet coincidentally out of town...why not? I'm caught up on my new book. Pete is in the clear." Sarah felt her smile widen. "We have the whole week to ourselves, June Bug."

"You bet we do, love," Amanda nearly exploded with joy. "Come on and let's get inside before we freeze our tushies off."

Sarah rubbed her backside one more time and then hurried into her coffee shop and out of the snow storm. The coffee shop was warm, smelled of coffee and cinnamon rolls, and welcomed Sarah with loving arms. "Oh, how I love this little place," Sarah told Amanda in a tender voice.

Amanda quickly closed the front door and began stomping snow off her white boots. "I do, too, love," she admitted.

Sarah looked around the cozy front room, admired the old-fashioned touches she and Amanda had insisted upon, and then slowly removed her pink coat, pink winter hat and pair of white insulated gloves. "I wish Pete were here," she sighed.

Amanda glanced over at Sarah. Her best friend looked so beautiful in the soft white and yellow winter dress she had bought recently at O'Mally's. Sure, the dress wasn't her typical style, and certainly not Sarah's usual practical dark colors, but Sarah had been in a spring kind of mood when she had chosen such soft colors for the day, and Amanda liked seeing the effect on her. She cared about her best friend's happiness. And to her relief, Sarah did seem truly happy—more than happy, she seemed content; even though a part of her heart would always remain in Los Angeles with Pete. "Pete did promise to visit," she pointed out.

Sarah turned and looked into Amanda's caring face. The woman was red from the cold, wearing a grizzly bear of a coat, a thick brown ski cap and gloves thick enough to keep an elephant warm—but underneath all the layers she knew there was a warm, loving, brave woman who Sarah loved more than life. "Boop," Sarah smiled and touched the tip of Amanda's nose.

"Boop to you," Amanda grinned and touched the tip of Sarah's nose back. "Now, let's make some coffee, love, before my blood turns to ice."

"You got it," Sarah replied and hurried into the kitchen as Amanda removed her coat, revealing a thick, green wool dress chosen for warmth rather than style. Amanda cared about fashion and style, but on stormy, snowy days when the temperature dipped low enough to freeze a penny to a hot stove, well, the need to stay warm defeated her desire to look stylish.

As Amanda removed her coat, the front door opened. Andrew came bursting in, his winter police parka covered in snow, and shivering all over. "Morning," he said through a stuffy nose.

"Shut the door quick," Amanda begged as a gust of icy wind grabbed at her face.

Andrew fought the door shut against the gust and began slapping snow off his coat. "Coffee ready?" he asked, sounding like a trombone stuck under water. The poor man was suffering from a terrible cold that threatened to turn into the flu—so was half of Snow Falls. Andrew ran the three-man police department even though he was barely able to show up for work himself. So far, Sarah and Amanda had managed to dodge the flu.

"You poor dear," said Amanda, "you sound worse today than you did yesterday."

Andrew removed a thick black ski cap with the state crest embroidered on the front and nodded. "I feel worse," he admitted. "Matthew called in on me. It's down to me and Nate."

"Oh dear," Amanda gasped.

Andrew walked over to a vintage coffee table and plopped down on his favorite cozy armchair with a view of the front windows, even though there was nothing to see but the swirling storm outside. "I could deputize some folks..." Andrew paused and anxiously glanced at Amanda.

"Oh no," Amanda exclaimed and threw her hands up in protest. "This is a girls' week! Los Angeles and I are going to spend this week shopping, eating brownies, painting our nails, complaining about our husbands...no way are we going to step foot in that awful police station."

Sarah heard the commotion from the kitchen and stepped into the front room. She spotted Andrew sagging over in his chair, looking like a sick grizzly bear as he slowly sunk down toward the floor. "Oh, Andrew, you should be home resting," she said with concern.

Andrew pulled a handkerchief out of his front pocket and blew his nose so loud that Amanda winced and delicately placed a box of tissues on the table in front of him. "Matthew called in sick," he told Sarah. "It's just me and Nate...and Nate ain't far off from being bedridden himself."

Amanda threw a desperate look at Sarah. "Andrew wants us to volunteer to wear the badge for a little while," she explained and begged Sarah to say no with her eyes.

"Conrad left town before the flu broke out," Andrew said, deliberately trying to guilt Sarah. The trick was underhanded and not very nice—but a sick man didn't have time to be nice; a sick man wanted a warm bed, a bowl of hot soup, a glass of orange juice, and sleep...lots and lots of sleep. "I think Conrad skipped out on me on purpose."

Deep down Sarah knew Andrew was right: he needed help. Conrad had hurried out of Snow Falls and rushed to New York to help an old friend. The truth was that Conrad was worried about catching the flu (or so he claimed) and jumped ship, leaving Sarah to deal with the panicked passengers. Sarah didn't mind her husband leaving town—she knew that Conrad needed a break from Snow Falls and from all the stress he had been under. What Sarah did mind was being left to deal with the fussy chief of police. "Andrew, we both know Conrad has been under a great deal of stress. Pete and I were nearly killed while trying to solve his case in Los Angeles. He just...needed a break from everything, right, June Bug?"

"Huh?" Amanda asked from her spot at the counter where she arranged fresh muffins in the display case. She quickly locked eyes with Sarah. "Oh...yeah, sure, your bloke sure needed to rest...a long rest. Yes indeed, poor bloke was on the verge of a nervous collapse...he needed a rest...just to rest, rest, rest and rest—"

Sarah nudged Amanda with her elbow. "I think Andrew

gets it, June Bug," she said in a desperate voice through a pained smile.

Andrew stared at Sarah and Amanda with sick, exhausted eyes. He loved the two women like they were his own sisters—his own blood relatives—but he wasn't in the mood to be trifled with. "Sarah...Detective Garland...I could be very nice and ask you to take over for me...or I could use my authority to force you to," he said, shoving his politeness out the door. "The city codes require me to have no less than two officers on duty at all times, and to deputize reserve members of the force if there are circumstances preventing us from meeting that quota." Andrew snuffled and forced his legs to stand up. "Detective Garland, I'm hereby putting you in charge until further notice." Andrew lifted a weak hand and pointed at Amanda. "I'm hereby making you an officer of the law until further notice...and...and..." Andrew stopped talking and began sneezing into his sleeve. When the sneezes stopped, he stumbled over to the front door. "Forget the coffee...I'm going home. Go down to the station...all the keys are in my desk...Nate is at his desk...send him home."

"But—" Amanda began to object.

"No buts," Andrew ordered and flung open the front door. "You're the only two healthy people left, I think. Perform your civic duty...and...just try not to burn the town down."

Sarah watched as Andrew pulled his black hat down on his head, shielded his face against a powerful wind, and then vanished back out into the storm. "I guess...our shopping trip is canceled," she sighed.

"Oh," Amanda said in a furious voice. She stomped one foot on the floor and braced her arms together tightly against her chest. "I could just...pow...right to the nose," she said, aiming her anger at Andrew.

"Well, the poor man is sick," Sarah pointed out and then let out a heavy moan. "And...he does have a duty to the town. Conrad did desert a sinking ship. I guess it is my responsibility to...perform my civic duty, as Andrew so nicely put it."

"Civic duty my foot," Amanda fussed and stomped her foot again. "He's just getting back at you...the fink."

"Conrad or Andrew?" Sarah asked.

"Both of them," Amanda growled. "If Conrad were here we wouldn't have to cancel our shopping trip." Amanda looked at Sarah and frowned. "I'm acting a bit silly, aren't I, love? After all, we did get caught up on our shopping while we were in Los Angeles, didn't we?"

"After Pete and I nabbed that lousy, good-for-nothing, rotten cop," Sarah nodded.

Amanda unfolded her arms. "After that lousy, good-for-nothing, rotten cop nearly killed you in that awful warehouse, let's not forget," she pointed out. "Poor Conrad...he's going to have a nervous breakdown before he's fifty."

Sarah winced. "I did put him through a scare, didn't I?"

"You and Pete vanished in the middle of the night," Amanda told Sarah in a pained voice. "We found you in an emergency room being treated for a concussion. Yes, love, I would say you put Conrad through an awful scare." Amanda shook her head. "I suppose...because I'm such a good-hearted person...I can't blame Conrad for needing a few days to himself."

Sarah began wondering if Conrad's excuse to leave town in order to escape the flu and all the stress he had been facing was true. Could it be, she worried, that her husband simply needed a break from her? "The virus...after the killer from England...that bad cop in Los Angeles that Pete and I tangled with..." she whispered. "Could I be the one running Conrad off?"

"Oh love," Amanda said and quickly put her hand on Sarah's shoulder, "you're not running Conrad off," she promised. "The man just needed to take a few days and catch his breath is all. Besides, we all know that Conrad hates being sick. Every time he gets a sniffle he drinks a sea of orange juice and runs to the doctor."

Sarah wasn't so sure. "But am I...doing to Conrad what I did to my first husband?" she asked in a hurt voice. *Yes...yes, you are...*a hideous snowman chewing on a candy cane taunted Sarah. *Conrad is going to divorce you, Sarah...leave you hanging high and dry...out in the cold...cold and frozen...*

"Love," Amanda told Sarah in a stern voice, shaking her friend out of her reverie, "Conrad isn't your first husband. Conrad is...as much as I would never say this to his face...he's a good man that is dedicated to his wife and to his marriage. He's so deeply in love with you, why, it would take a million...no...a trillion lifetimes to pry him just a simple inch away from you." Amanda smiled and touched Sarah's nose. "You tell that nasty snowman voice in your mind to go suck an egg and stop worrying about Conrad."

"Do you really think Conrad doesn't mind?" Sarah asked as tears began to swell up in her throat. Before Amanda could answer she turned away, wiped at her eyes, and then looked down at her nervous hands. "Go away," she told the hideous snowman, "you can't hurt me anymore...go away...my husband is committed to me and I'm committed to him...so just...go away!"

Amanda looked at Sarah's back with worried eyes and began wondering what words of comfort she might give. She tried to voice her concerns and reassurances but was interrupted when Mitchel Cochran stumbled through the front door with his ratty old cane in one hand and the morning paper in the other. "Coffee ready?" he asked in his usual gruff voice.

Sarah turned around, spotted Mitchel, and then hurried to close the front door. "Mr. Cochran, you should be dressed warmer," she said in an alarmed voice.

Mitchel wasn't in the mood to be scolded by a woman young enough to be his daughter. He was an eighty-year-old man who was still tough enough to tangle with a grumpy grizzly bear. "I ain't worried about a few snowflakes falling from the sky, Sarah Garland," he snapped. "I've lived in Alaska my entire life." Mitch shook his head in disgust and wandered over to his usual table. "Young folks today think the world will end if it starts snowing...enough to make a man lose sleep," he fussed. "Ruin a man's morning paper, too."

Amanda looked at Sarah and grinned. She loved Mitchel very deeply and knew that the old man was one of a kind. "I guess I'll keep the shop open while you walk down to the station," she told Sarah.

Sarah watched Mitchel shrug off what appeared to be nothing more than a thin green windbreaker and toss it down on the floor next to his chair. "He's wearing nothing more than a spring jacket and a long sleeve button-up shirt," she worried aloud. "He'll catch his death." Her worries about her husband still played about in her mind as she looked on as Mitch settled in to read his paper grumpily.

Amanda locked her eyes on Mitchel and smiled. "Love,

half of the people in Snow Falls are sick with the flu. That old man is out and about in this snow, healthy as a butterfly in a warm breeze. I don't think we have to worry about him."

Mitchel raised his hard face and looked at Sarah. "Are you going to serve me my coffee or am I going to have to take my business elsewhere?"

"Oh, stop fussing and hush," Amanda scolded Mitchel. "You just read your paper and mind your manners or I'll kick you out of here. You know darn well we brew the best coffee in town and that's why you keep coming here, you old goat."

Mitchel mumbled something, snatched off his red and black hunting cap, rattled open his newspaper to another section, and went on reading. "I guess I'll go to the station and send Nate home," Sarah told Amanda as a sweet smile replaced her fear of losing Conrad. She watched Mitch as he perused the paper with a frown and a squint. "He is something, isn't he?"

"The old-timers always are," Amanda smiled back at Sarah. "I'll hurry to his coffee and see you at the diner around lunch."

"Deal," Sarah promised and quickly put on her coat, ski hat, and gloves, and slipped outside into the snowstorm. The world outside was frozen, white and silent aside from the winds howling through the mountains and trees around them. Not a person or vehicle was moving. For a moment Sarah stood very still, absorbing the frozen beauty covering Snow Falls. "My beautiful life," she whispered, "let's just keep it beautiful, can we?" She carefully walked through the icy snowbanks to the police station not knowing that a murder—a very unusual murder—was about to take place on her watch.

Chapter Two

Sarah walked into Conrad's office, closed the door, and then eased down behind his desk on cold legs. "I wish you were here, honey," she whispered. A photo of Sarah and Conrad in front of the old lone cabin in the untamed wilderness was perched on Conrad's desk. Sarah looked at the photo, remembering that day, studying Conrad's smiling face filled with love and peace, and sighed. "Oh Conrad, I hope I'm not running you off," she said and then studied her own face. "We were so happy that day. I look very happy...and so does Conrad. We belong together."

Nate knocked on the office door, stuck his face into the office, and said in a miserable, sick voice: "Okay, Sarah, I'm all cleaned up. The morning reports are finished and filed away."

"Oh, I would have worked on the morning reports," Sarah assured Nate.

"More habit than necessity," Nate explained and then blew his nose into a yellow handkerchief. The poor man looked horrible. "It's just a few questions I fill out, then stamp with the department seal and file away. Not much to it. Been doing the same report for years. Anyway, if it's okay I think I'll go on home. Becky made me some soup and I'm dying on my feet here."

"Of course," Sarah told Nate, "but before you go, I need to ask you a few quick questions."

"Shoot," Nate said and leaned against the door jam tiredly.

"How long will the plows be keeping the main road clear?"

"Old Steve will plow the main street every half hour or so and keep making his rounds until he gets hungry for lunch. Then he'll run a few more rounds...oh, probably until three or so when it gets really dark, and then go on home."

Sarah didn't know Steve very well but felt grateful the man ran his snow plow for the town, and on his own dime and time, too. "When will the schools reopen?" she asked.

"As soon as this storm ends and the mayor decides to pay a few more people to start plowing the roads," Nate explained. "Mr. Walnut will give you a call."

"Mr. Walnut is—?"

"Superintendent. Mr. Walnut oversees the elementary, middle and high school," Nate told Sarah. "All three schools are located in one building...not much to it, really. Snow Falls isn't Anchorage, you know. You could count the last graduating class on one hand."

Sarah smiled. "I guess you're right."

"Any more questions?" Nate asked.

"All the important phone numbers?"

Nate pointed to Conrad's desk. "Top left hand drawer."

"Got it," Sarah replied and then frowned: "Emergency calls?"

Nate let out a deep breath. "Sarah, like I said, we live in a small town. Snow Falls doesn't have a 911 dispatcher or call center like the larger places do. All calls come straight in to the station. That's why it's required that one officer be on duty at the station at all times, and one other be available to make rounds, if the roads are passable." Nate fought back a round of coughs. "You and Amanda are going to have to take turns."

"I was afraid of that," Sarah told Nate and then let out a tired smile. "Maybe I should go around town and slap a badge on every healthy person I see?"

"Wish you could," Nate told Sarah. "But every person Andrew slaps a badge on has to be reported to the state and then there's a background check—"

"All the red tape. I understand."

Nate nodded. "It's a headache to deputize a new local onto the force. It's not like Andy deputizing Floyd the barber while he goes on a picnic with Helen Crump—Floyd retired from the force, you'll recall, so he's on the level with the state," he explained. "New folks are lots of paperwork and a whole bunch of useless questions. You and Amanda, though, you're all set." Nate looked at Sarah with grateful eyes. "You're a cop, Sarah. We'll all feel safer with you at the station manning the helm. If Andrew had grabbed a local, he would have had to stay at the station. Can't leave an untrained local alone, you know."

"I'm glad to be...performing my civic duty," Sarah tried to joke but she could tell Nate wasn't in the mood for a joke. The poor man was slap happy with fatigue and ready to punch out. "Go home, Nate. I can cover the station until Andrew feels better."

"Thanks, Sarah," Nate said and managed a weak smile. "Call Andrew first if anything goes wrong, okay?"

"I promise."

Nate waved a weak hand in the air and shuffled away, leaving Sarah all alone to manage the station. "Well," Sarah said and began tapping her right finger on Conrad's desk as the winds howled and screamed outside, "what to do...what to do?" Sarah looked at the phone sitting on the desk. "I really should call Conrad and let him know—" Before Sarah could finish her sentence the phone rang. "Oh..." she said in a startled voice and answered the call. "Hello...uh...Detective Garland...I mean, Detective Spencer speaking."

"Detective Sarah Spencer, I like that," Conrad's voice floated into Sarah's ears from the Bronx.

"Oh, Conrad, I was just getting ready to call you," Sarah exclaimed in an excited voice. "I was—"

"Thinking about me?" Conrad smiled, standing in a small, stuffy apartment, staring at a man with a pair of binoculars in his hands, watching through the window.

"Well...yes," Sarah blushed. "I miss you."

"I was thinking about you, too," Conrad promised Sarah, turning his back to the man. "Amanda told me you were at the station. What's going on?"

"Everyone is sick and I've been deputized...nominated to perform my civic duty," Sarah explained and then let out a little laugh. "Andrew and Nate just went home. I'm...solo until Amanda arrives. Uh...how are things in New York?"

Conrad listened to a hard, cold rain falling and then closed his eyes. "I'm on a stakeout," he whispered. "My buddy Jack...isn't doing so good, Sarah. He's being framed. Unless we catch the people framing him, he could lose his job and his pension into the bargain."

"Oh my," Sarah said. "Is there anything I can do?"

"Pray," Conrad replied. "Pray we catch them before it's too late."

"Of course."

"And," Conrad added, "since you're at the station, maybe you can run a few names for me?"

"Absolutely," Sarah promised and grabbed a pen and piece of paper. "I'm ready for the names, honey."

"Honey?" Conrad whispered, "you don't know how sweet...how your voice...how...oh. how I wish I were home with you."

"Conrad, is something the matter?" Sarah asked in a worried voice.

"Yes," Conrad confessed. "I...well, Sarah, I didn't tell you the whole truth about my trip."

"The truth?" Sarah asked, feeling her heart sink. Surely Conrad was going to express his desire to divorce her—end their marriage—and leave Snow Falls. His former life as a detective in New York City was calling him, she just knew it.

"Sarah, I hate getting sick, but that's not the reason I left Snow Falls," Conrad began to explain as his friend Jack lit a cigar.

"Why then?" Sarah asked.

Conrad glanced at Jack. "To help Jack."

"You told me about Jack."

"But I didn't tell you that someone was out to kill him, Sarah," Conrad explained. "And it's more than that. I'm afraid that whoever is out to kill Jack might have connected me to him...and then try to harm you to get to me and Jack. I left Snow Falls because...I was scared for you." Conrad ran his left hand through his hair. "I know you're one tough cop, Sarah...the best, in my book...and maybe I did act like an over-protective husband...but you've been through so much already and I was scared for you—"

"Stop," Sarah begged as tears began to fall from her eyes, "you don't need to say another word."

Conrad heard Sarah begin to cry. "Sarah...baby...I didn't mean to upset you."

"These are tears of relief," Sarah promised. "I was...so afraid you left Snow Falls because you wanted to...leave me."

"Leave you?" Conrad asked in a shocked voice.

"I've...put you through so many stressful situations," Sarah explained, allowing her tears to fall. "I was scared you became upset with me in Los Angeles. I didn't mean to vanish on you...and cause you worry, but Pete received an urgent call and we had to act. I wanted to call you, but we didn't have time and—"

"Sarah," Conrad interrupted in a confused voice, "why would I get upset? We're cops. I understand how vital it is to act when the door opens. You explained everything to me at the time. Sometimes all we have is a split second to catch the bad guys."

"I was nearly killed, and I thought you—"

"Honey," Conrad said in a soft, loving voice, "that's all part of the job. I would never want to end our marriage because you risked your life to save others. I mean...if I ever lost you my life would be over...but I can't put you in a cage. I wanted to keep you safe after you and Amanda nearly died at the hot springs, but I realized that if I tried to pen you up somewhere...I would lose you." Conrad saw Sarah's sweet and beautiful face whisper into his mind. "Honey, you're an amazing cop, writer and woman, and I love you for you who are. I can't slap chains on you any more than you can on me. I mean, look at me, I'm on a stakeout trying to track down some very dangerous people. Does that mean you're going to end our marriage?"

"Of course not," Sarah promised, shocked.

"Exactly," Conrad continued. "I love you, Sarah, and I know that you love me. We belong together and that's a fact. You're my...soul mate."

"You're my soul mate," Sarah whispered as fresh tears rolled down her cheeks.

Conrad closed his eyes again. "Sarah, I called because I wanted to hear your voice...and because you're the only person I can trust right now. I'm sure I could trust Andrew, but he has a lot on his plate right now. I knew it was time to stop keeping you in the dark about what's going on and bring you on board."

"I'm on board," Sarah promised. "I'll run the names you gave me and call you—"

"No," Conrad quickly interrupted. "Don't call me. Just in case. I'll call you tomorrow around this time, okay?"

"Hey, we have movement," Conrad's friend called out.

"Honey, I have to go. I'll call you tomorrow."

"Okay...love you," Sarah promised Conrad.

"Love you more than life," Conrad answered back and ended the call.

Sarah slowly put down the phone, wiped at her tears and then looked down at the names she had written down. Then the phone rang again. Sarah snatched up the phone: "Conrad?"

"Los Angeles, this is Amanda," Amanda told Sarah in a scared voice. "You better get back to the coffee shop."

"I'm supposed to be manning the phones for emergency calls, I can't leave. What's the matter?"

"Mitchel Cochran is dead," Amanda told Sarah, peeking her head out of the kitchen toward the dining room of the café. "I went to refill his coffee and...his face was down on the table, next to his coffee. I thought the old guy had fallen asleep...I checked his pulse...he's dead." Amanda let out a scared whimper.

"Heart attack?" Sarah asked, her mind racing.

"I don't know," Amanda said, "but what I do know is that there are three old women standing over Mitchel's body. I don't know who they are. They were standing over his body when I went out to refill his coffee. I barely got past them to check his pulse. It was so awkward. I don't feel safe here with them and they won't leave. Oh, Los Angeles, hurry and get over here." Amanda shivered all over and lowered her voice to the smallest possible whisper. "I think those old bats killed Mitchel."

Sarah bit down on her lip. She wasn't supposed to leave the station unmanned, but what choice did she have? "I'm on my way."

"Hurry."

"You bet." Sarah slammed down the phone, grabbed her gloves, and raced outside into the snow. The storm greeted her with an angry howl and the winds pelted heavy snow into her face. Sarah ignored the snow and icy winds, slapped on her gloves and snow hat, and carefully aimed her body toward the coffee shop. "It has to be a heart attack," she reassured herself, trudging through deep snow. As she worked through the snow, Sarah let her eyes wander around. Not a single person was in sight. The main street was covered with white, clean snowdrifts, piled at the edges where the snow plow had passed through. Only a few daring businesses remained open and only a handful of tough trucks were parked in the snow. "It has to be a heart attack...Mr. Cochran is an old man..." But who were these old women in her coffee shop hovering around the body, and what did they know? What had they done?

Sarah finally reached the coffee shop door, pushed her way inside, and, sure enough, there stood the three women over Mitchel Cochran's body, chatting away in lowered voices. All three women were in their early to mid-seventies, dressed in winter clothing and dusted with snow; like Mitchel, the cold didn't seem to bother them one little bit, judging from their lack of heavy winter attire. "Uh...good morning, ladies. What seems to be the problem here?" Sarah asked, pushing the front door closed behind her. The women turned to look at her, all three pairs of eyes unblinking and staring at the same time.

Before any of the three women could answer Sarah, Amanda burst out of the kitchen, grabbed Sarah's arm, and dragged her back toward the kitchen. "Those three women have been standing over the body this entire time," she explained in a creeped-out voice. "Like vultures..."

Sarah peeked her head through the kitchen door and studied the three women standing over Mitchel's body and craning their necks to look at the kitchen where Sarah and Amanda had vanished. "Maybe I should question them?" she asked. "We can't be rude and stay back here, Amanda. You're safe with me now." Sarah patted the gun safe in her ankle holster.

"I...guess," Amanda winced.

"Come on." Sarah took Amanda's hand and walked her back into the main room. "Ladies, my name is Detective

Garland...Spencer." She realized she recognized the women as the O'Healey sisters. Rarely seen around town, Abigail, Martha and Betty were known as somewhat eccentric. Sarah wracked her mind trying to remember the last time she had seen them out and about. It had been some time. She stepped forward confidently. "I'm afraid I'm going to have to ask you to stand back. I need to examine the...body."

"Why?" Abigail O'Healey asked. "Mitchel is dead."

"Oh, yes, he's dead," Martha O'Healey confirmed.

"Oh yes, indeed," Betty O'Healey added, "Mitchel is dead."

"Uh...do you ladies know how he died?" Sarah dared to ask, taken aback by their chorusing voices, seemingly identical and almost in a sing-song tone.

"Of course we do," Abigail told Sarah in a proud voice that wavered only a little with age.

"How?" Sarah asked.

"We killed him," Martha answered.

"We had no other choice," Betty added. "It was time."

"Oh yes, it was time," Abigail said, and Martha nodded. "We waited far too long."

Sarah's stomach felt colder than a brick of ice at hearing their matter-of-fact words, so chilling and creepy. She glanced at Amanda. Amanda shrugged her shoulders. "Crazy old bats," she whispered.

Sarah winced. She did not for a second believe the women had actually killed Mitchel. What a mess. "Uh...ladies...I've seen some of you in Snow Falls—"

"We live in Snow Falls during the winters," Abigail informed Sarah primly. "In our cabin located at 89 Whitebridge Road."

"Whitebridge Road isn't too far from town," Amanda said, glancing at Sarah.

"We like to stay close," Betty explained.

"Very close," Martha added.

Amanda looked at them in confusion, then back at her friend. "Arrest them, love."

Sarah drew in a deep breath. "Uh...ladies, how did you kill Mr. Cochran?" she asked.

"Oh, we can't tell you that," Betty told Sarah.

"Never," Martha agreed.

"Our secret will go to the grave," Abigail finished.

"Uh...well," Sarah struggled to speak, "because you confessed to killing this man...I have no other choice but to place you under arrest." She shrugged at Amanda, knowing she would have to explain later. If these women were indeed mentally ill, or perhaps senile with age, an investigation would surely turn up evidence one way or another as to how Mitchel had actually died.

Abigail, Martha and Betty turned and looked at Sarah, unblinking again. "We said we killed him...but we didn't say it was our hands that did the killing," Abigail explained.

"No, our hands did not kill Mitchel," Martha confirmed.

"Our hands are clean," Betty added and then looked down at Mitchel. "But we did kill Mitchel, nonetheless. What choice did we have?"

"No choice," Abigail and Martha consoled Betty. "We waited far too long to begin with."

Sarah felt confusion grip her mind. She didn't have time to untangle the ramblings of three old women. Conrad was in danger and needed her help. However, a man was dead, which meant an investigation would have to be opened. Surely they would need to call for a forensic psychologist from Anchorage to determine the truth anyway, so all Sarah had to worry about was keeping them safe and preserving the evidence. She sighed hugely. "Okay, ladies," Sarah said, "I'm afraid I have no choice. You're going to have to come down to the station with me."

"Police work," Abigail whispered loudly to Martha and Betty. "I've seen it on the Perry Mason show. We're suspects."

"Oh, how exciting," Martha and Betty whispered to each other.

"Isn't it?" Abigail whispered back and clapped her hands together.

Amanda stepped up to Sarah. "Love, you better call the people who run the padded room-type hospitals," she said. "Does Conrad keep any straitjackets in the station?"

"I don't know...I just..." Sarah tried to form a coherent thought but couldn't speak. All she could do was stare at the three old women standing over Mitchel's body and wonder what in the world was going on.

Chapter Three

Marching three old ladies through a snow storm over icy sidewalks covered in snow wasn't an easy task. The storm was growing worse but, to her relief and delight, Old Steve was keeping the main street clear; for the time being, at least. "Are you ladies okay?" Sarah called over an icy wind.

Abigail touched the lapels of her old fashioned brown peacoat that draped down to a pair of old snow boots. "We're fine, dear," she answered and smoothed down a furry winter hat covering her short gray hair. It looked like real fur, and from its vintage look Sarah guessed it might be mink, or perhaps beaver. The older woman stood up straight and marched through the snow with purpose. "I've lived through more winters than you've been alive, and so has this hat."

"We all have," Betty pointed out, bravely walking through the snow with her gray coat open and flapping in the wind. The poor woman should have been frozen, yet she seemed content in her simple winter coat, which was white and boxy and came down nearly to her narrow calves. She also wore a white fringed wool scarf and a white winter hat. "Our parents took us to the Yukon Territory in our youth many times. As for me, the cold and I are very old friends. My sisters would all say the same."

"Indeed," Martha agreed. Martha, like her two sisters, displayed no concern about the cold. She wore a green wool frock coat with a pale cream ruff of fur along the lapels, a matching green hat, and a loosely knotted wool scarf flapped in the wind around her. Her coat was not even buttoned. The woman, although thin and fragile in appearance, was obviously very tough. "You kids today wouldn't have survived in the old days."

Abigail let out a chuckle. "Kids today can't live without them gadgets they're always playing with. In our day," she said, pausing in front of a bakery and studying a delicious plate of muffins in the display window, "we played outside in the woods, became acquainted with the wildlife, bathed in the river and climbed trees."

Sarah hugged her coat tighter around her. "Where...exactly...are you ladies from?" she asked as snow pelted her frozen face.

"The northern territories of the Alaska interior," Martha explained. "Our papa was a lumber man and a hunter. Born in Alaska after the Gold Rush, you know."

"The Gold Rush?" Sarah asked, confused. "Wasn't that… quite some time ago?"

"Of course, dear," Abigail replied. But from her suddenly thin lips and glances at her sisters, Sarah realized she had made a mistake to refer to the sisters' ages so blatantly.

"Well, you must love Alaska very much," Sarah said, trying to salvage the conversation and still hoping the sisters would reveal some clue as to the death of Mitchel Cochran. "What brought you to this little town?"

"Why, where one sister goes, the others must follow," Abigail smiled, ignoring the cold striking her wrinkled face. This did not quite answer the question, but all three sisters smiled enigmatically and seemed to think they had explained themselves fully.

Sarah let out a low moan. "Uh...well, that's...nice."

"I'm sorry we haven't met before today's...uh...tragic events," Sarah said. She thought quickly about a more polite way to ask about their age. "Who is the eldest sister?"

"I'm the oldest," Abigail explained. "I'm seventy-five. Betty is seventy-three and Martha is the baby."

"I'm only seventy-one," Martha smiled at Sarah. "Mother had me late in life. The poor dear was twenty-two years old."

"Twenty-two...late in life?" Sarah asked. "I...well, I...suppose that could be considered late."

"Have you any children, dear?" Abigail asked Sarah, studying the woman's eyes. She saw a special light—a goodness—in Sarah that pleased her heart.

"Uh...no," Sarah answered in a painful voice. "I was never blessed with children."

"Oh," Betty and Martha exclaimed in matching sad tones, "we're so sorry to hear that. Children are such a beautiful gift from the Lord."

"I have five children," Abigail told Sarah as the snow continued to fall. "Betty has four children. Baby sister Martha has five children."

"Mostly boys, but a few girls," Betty explained.

"And lots and lots of beautiful grandchildren," Martha beamed.

"Indeed," Abigail smiled. "When we get the time, we leave the territory and go see our families."

"All of our children live south of the snow line," Betty explained. "They prefer the warmth. We like the cold."

"Papa and Mother are buried in the northern territory and someday," Abigail told Sarah, "my sisters and I will be buried next to them." She nodded happily as if looking forward to her own death.

Sarah shuddered. She glanced around at the deserted main street. "We better get to the station."

Abigail nodded politely and continued walking. Betty and Martha followed like two women simply taking an afternoon stroll in a sunny park.

When Sarah reached the station, she carefully ushered the three women inside and closed the front door. "Amanda is watching the body," she explained. "Doctor Milton will be by soon, after he checks on a patient of his who is nursing a broken leg. I'm going to have to go back to my coffee shop when Dr. Milton arrives. But in the meantime, I need to ask you ladies a few questions."

"Oh, just like Perry Mason," Abigail beamed.

"Uh...yes," Sarah said and pointed toward Conrad's office. She could not fathom ushering this trio of oddball ladies into an interrogation room, and in any case, they did not strike her as dangerous in any way, shape, or form. "If you please," she said, holding open the door for them.

Abigail, Betty and Martha all clapped their hands in delight and walked into Conrad's office like three excited children preparing to ride a roller coaster for the first time. "This is so much fun," Abigail said and quickly sat down in one of the two chairs facing Conrad's desk and removed her hat. "Betty, you sit down next to me. Martha, dear, you sit in that chair over there in the corner."

"Oh no, she can have this chair," Sarah said and pulled Conrad's office chair out from behind the desk and stationed it for Martha. "I'll sit on the edge of the desk."

Martha smiled at Sarah. "So polite," she said, sitting down. "All the policemen in Snow Falls are polite."

"Indeed," Betty agreed, sitting down next to Abigail. "Very friendly people."

"Sure," Sarah replied. She slowly removed her ski cap and set it beside her on the desk. Her recent misadventures in Los Angeles weighed heavily on her mind and she could not stop herself from adding a few words. "Ladies, there are some very bad and crooked cops in this world. You can't trust a person simply because he or she is a cop. Cops are the bad guys sometimes, too." She sighed, remembering everything she had been through lately.

"Oh my," Martha gasped, "we didn't know that."

"Indeed," Betty exclaimed. "That is horrible news."

"Tragic," Abigail tutted. "We thought all officers were good people."

"Not all of them, I'm afraid," Sarah explained, assuming she was simply informing three old women about a sad reality of the real world. Instead, she'd created an unforeseen problem that Conrad would end up laughing about for years, because it would turn out the three sisters were more taken by this piece of information than she ever could have guessed. "Now—"

"Just a minute, dear," Abigail said in a serious voice and quickly motioned her sisters over. Sarah wrinkled her brow as the three women huddled together and began whispering to one another.

After a couple of minutes passed, Abigail looked up at Sarah with curious eyes. Even though she saw good in Sarah, it seemed obvious the woman couldn't be trusted, after her little announcement about crooked police; or so Abigail's confused and excitable mind believed. "I saw on a Perry Mason show a man was told he didn't have to talk to the police if he didn't want to. Is that true?" she asked in a careful voice.

"Well, you don't have to answer my questions unless—well, listen, you're not under arrest yet. Not technically. If you were, I would read you your rights and say something like 'you have the right to remain silent' and—"

"We wish to remain silent," Abigail announced.

"Indeed," Betty agreed.

"We do not want to talk to bad cops," Martha added and made a sour face at Sarah.

Sarah stared at the three women in shock. "Ladies, I'm not a bad cop," she said in a desperate voice. "I was only telling you before—"

"That you can't be trusted," Abigail cut Sarah off and then looked at her sisters. Her face flushed with excitement. "Oh, this is too fun," she giggled. "We're trapped in the snow with one of the bad guys from Perry Mason!"

"Ladies, I'm not a bad person. I was simply trying to explain that not all cops are good," Sarah begged in a strained voice.

"Indeed," Betty said and pointed at Sarah. "You were very kind to inform us that you yourself are not to be trusted."

"But that's not...I—"

"We appreciate your honesty, dear," Abigail told Sarah firmly and offered her a warm smile. "Honesty is very important."

"Papa said a dishonest person is worse than a snake in the grass," Martha explained. "As it says in Proverbs, whoever takes a crooked path will be found out."

"But I was explaining about..." Sarah stopped talking, let out a heavy sigh, and then looked down at the coating of snow slowly melting off of her winter coat. "Why me?" she mumbled and sat silent for a minute. Finally, she raised her head. "Ladies, a man is dead. You admitted to killing him."

"Not with our hands, dear," Abigail explained and then quickly covered her mouth. "Oh, I'm not remaining silent, am I?"

"No, you're not," Betty replied.

"Afraid not," Martha agreed and looked at Sarah. "Please, stop talking. We don't want to tell this person anything."

"But I have to ask you a few questions," Sarah insisted. "A man is dead."

Abigail, Betty and Martha quickly huddled together again and began whispering. After a few minutes Abigail poked her head up into the air. "Dear, on the Perry Mason show we watched, a man demanded he be given a phone call to call...one of them...law men."

"Lawyer is the word the bad man used on the show," Betty quickly explained to Abigail. Abigail beamed and patted Betty's arm. "You were always the smart one," she said. Betty blushed.

Sarah rubbed the bridge of her nose. "Yes, ladies, you can contact a lawyer. Once you're under arrest."

Abigail, Betty and Martha clapped their hands in victory. "Oh, this is so much fun," they said.

"Who is your lawyer?" Sarah asked, too overwhelmed to explain once again that they were not under arrest yet.

"Our lawyer?" Abigail asked.

"Yes, who is your lawyer?" Sarah asked again. "You do have a lawyer, don't you?"

Abigail frowned. "I'm afraid we don't, dear. Isn't that your job? Don't you have a Perry Mason type person we can use?"

Sarah moaned again. "Snow Falls doesn't have a public defender," she explained.

"What is a public defender, dear?" Abigail asked.

Sarah closed her eyes. "Give me strength," she begged. Before she could say another word the telephone on Conrad's desk rang. "Excuse me for a minute," she told the sisters. "Hello, this is Detective Garland...I mean, Spencer, speaking. How may I help you?"

"Doc called me," Andrew's voice came over the phone, thick with phlegm and fatigue. "What's going on, Sarah?"

"Oh, Andrew, I'm so glad it's you," Sarah said in a relieved voice. "I was going to call you."

"Doc said Mitchel Cochran is dead?" Andrew asked from his spot on a soft and warm couch covered with a blanket. He reached out his right arm, took a glass of orange juice from a wooden dinner tray, and took a sip.

"It's nothing to worry about, Andrew," Sarah promised. "I have three...suspects...at the station as we speak."

"Suspects? Three of them?" Andrew asked as his weary eyes looked at his beautiful stone fireplace holding a roaring fire. He sure loved his cabin—the smell of pine and peppermint— and surely wasn't interested in going back out into the storm. Besides, he had on his special warm socks that were making his feet all nice and cozy.

"Yes, three...three women in their early to mid-seventies,"

Sarah explained, looking at the supposed killers sitting before her. What vicious killers they were, too, Sarah sighed.

Andrew put down his orange juice. "Sarah, are you talking about the O'Healey sisters?" he asked in a shocked voice.

"Yes, do you know them?" Sarah explained. "I was trying to get a few answers, but it's proving…difficult." She looked at Abigail. "Your last name is O'Healey, correct?" she asked.

"Yes, of course," Abigail smiled. "My last name by marriage is O'Healey."

"My name by marriage is O'Healey, too," Betty smiled.

"And my name by marriage is O'Healey as well," Martha finished.

"We married three Irish brothers working the land," Abigail explained. "Our maiden name came from Papa's family. Papa's last name was Greenlight and mother's last name was Wallace. Papa's folks were from the old country and came over in—"

"You can tell me your family history later, I promise," Sarah told Abigail and offered her a kind smile and focused back on the phone call. "Yes, Andrew, I have the three O'Healey sisters in front of me."

"And you think they killed Mitchel Cochran?" Andrew asked in a shocked voice. "Sarah, did you fall and hit your head? Or did they hit their heads, perhaps?"

Sarah turned her back to the three sisters and whispered in a frustrated voice. "Andrew, they admitted to killing the man. What was I supposed to do? It's standard procedure to question someone even if we don't think they—"

"I know, I know," Andrew replied. Even though he felt awful, a smile touched his face. "The O'Healey sisters…oh, this is good," he said and then sneezed all over himself.

"They admitted to killing Mitchel Cochran," Sarah repeated.

"Sarah, the O'Healey sisters are harmless. Every winter they come back to town and every spring they go south to visit their children. Why they come in the worst of the winter weather I'll never understand. They've always been a tad… different, I guess you could say. But they're good people. Why, the O'Healey brothers helped build Snow Falls back in the old days."

"Andrew, I don't care if the O'Healey brothers helped build the entire southern hemisphere. The O'Healey sisters confessed to a murder and it's my duty to investigate," Sarah grumbled in a voice that let Andrew know he was making an annoyed woman very, very mad. And if there was one truth Andrew knew and lived by, it was that you didn't make a woman mad unless you wanted to face dire consequences. He was smarter than that, or at least he hoped so.

"Maybe I should come down to the station," Andrew offered, even though his body was aching and moaning.

"Andrew, I dealt with the Back Alley Killer. I think I can handle three old ladies," Sarah replied and rolled her eyes. "The O'Healey sisters aren't exactly vicious killers."

"Maybe not," Andrew said and fought back a grin, "but all the old-timers in town know that Mitchel Cochran's people had a running feud with the Greenlights."

"A feud?" Sarah challenged him, disbelieving. "As in…a hillbilly 'your cow knocked over my fence' kinda feud?"

Andrew bit down on his lip to hold back laughter. It was clear that Sarah was annoyed, and he didn't want Sarah to come over to his cabin and shoot him. "Uh…no," he said. "Years back, way back in the old days, Matthew Greenlight claimed that Billy Cochran trespassed on his claim, dug up some gold, and stole it."

Sarah turned around and focused on Abigail, Betty and Martha, who were still whispering among themselves and ignoring her. "Okay, Andrew, I'm all ears. Tell me all that you know."

"Well," Andrew explained, "I did do a little digging myself...out of curiosity...when I was in my early twenties. It's quite the story. But you should know—" Before Andrew could finish, the call went dead in Sarah's hand.

Andrew heard the sound of a crashing tree just before the phone line cut out in the middle of his call. "Honey," he yelled in a scratchy voice, "that old tree just knocked out the phone line."

"What about Sarah?" a sweet voice called from a warm room.

Andrew put down the phone in his hand and began laughing. "I think Sarah is going to have a fun day with the O'Healey sisters."

Chapter Four

Sarah lowered the phone. "Guess the phone went out," she said. "I better try the coffee shop."

"We're in no rush, dear," Abigail smiled.

Sarah nodded and called Amanda. Amanda picked up on the first ring. "Where is Doctor Milton?" she begged.

"It takes a while to fix a broken leg, June Bug," Sarah told her frantic friend. "I was talking to Andrew and then the call went...dead. I'm just making sure the phones are working in this area."

Amanda peeked her head out of the back office. "I know Mitchel was an old man...but now he's a dead body...and dead bodies are creepy."

"Doctor Milton should be arriving soon," Sarah promised. "When he arrives, I'll walk back down to the coffee shop."

"Why did I get stuck watching a dead body?" Amanda complained. "I thought we were both deputized. Aren't we sisters?"

"We are, we are," Sarah promised. Even though she felt frustrated, the absurdity of Amanda babysitting a dead body made her smile. "June Bug, just lock the door and sit tight, you'll be fine. You're an amazing woman."

"Don't try to flatter me," Amanda griped and hurried back into the office and closed the door. "You're not going to get out of buying me an entirely new wardrobe."

"Deal," Sarah promised. "I'll be over when Dr. Milton arrives."

"I'll call you as soon as I hear his truck pull up," Amanda assured Sarah.

"Thanks, June Bug." Sarah hung up the phone, leaving Amanda stranded with a dead body, and focused back on Abigail, Betty and Martha. "Ladies—"

"We want to remain silent," Abigail reminded Sarah. "We can't trust you, remember?"

Sarah sighed. "Okay, okay," she said and held both hands up into the air, "I get it."

"You're a very smart woman," Martha smiled. "My sisters and I can plainly see that you are very smart."

"Indeed," Betty agreed. "We read all about you in the local paper and saw you on the news. You're a very popular woman."

"The people of Snow Falls are very impressed with you," Abigail explained and then added in a careful voice: "However, dear, some people are very weary of you. They claim that you have brought only trouble to Snow Falls."

Sarah didn't know what to say. It was no secret that many people in Snow Falls respected her and accepted her as their own. It was also no secret that many people in Snow Falls desired for her to move far, far away and leave them alone. Trouble had its way of following her no matter where she went. "People have the right to have their opinions of me," she finally spoke, "as long as their opinion is peaceful and nonviolent."

"Oh, indeed," Betty nodded. "There is far too much violence in this world."

Sarah drew in a deep breath. "Speaking of violence...can we please talk about Mitchel Cochran—"

"Oh, no you don't," Abigail gently scolded Sarah, "my sisters and I are remaining silent."

"Indeed," Betty said and folded her arms.

"Indeed we are," Martha agreed and followed suit.

Sarah felt like drowning her head in a cold river. Instead, she walked to the office door. "I'm going to get a cup of coffee. You ladies can join me if you would like."

"Oh no," Abigail told Sarah, "we only drink our own coffee that we make at home."

"We order our coffee straight from a coffee plantation way down there in South America," Martha told Sarah in a proud voice. "My son knows many different kinds of people from his travels and began bringing me coffee years ago from a man he met in Colombia. We all drink it." Martha patted Abigail and Betty's hands with love. "My sisters and I are very close."

"Indeed we are," Betty smiled.

"Indeed we are," Abigail agreed and gently patted Martha's hand. "My sisters and I share the same heart. We're inseparable."

Sarah felt a very warm and loving feeling cover her own heart. The love Abigail, Betty and Martha shared for one another was more special than anyone could put into words— the love ran deep and long, back through years and years of life that had created a bond of love that today's world could not and would never understand. Despite the strange events of the day, their love and loyalty touched her heart deeply. "Ladies," she said, "I...I think I'll go get a cup of coffee."

"We'll be here when you get back, dear," Abigail promised.

Sarah nodded and left Conrad's office. She made her way through the deserted police station to the coffee machine, picked up a mug, and filled it with hot coffee. Then she leaned against the wood-paneled wall next to the coffee counter and listened to the storm howl and cry outside. "How did they possibly kill him?" she asked in a low whisper. "They're too sweet. And possibly confused. His body showed no signs of violence...they said they killed him...but didn't touch him...poison?" Sarah spoke, tossing questions and concerns into the warm air. "Dr. Milton will tell me if Mitchel Cochran was poisoned...and if he was..." Sarah glanced toward Conrad's office. "How can I arrest those three sweet women? Murder is murder...but..." Sarah shook her head. "My goodness," she said and sipped at her coffee.

After Sarah finished half of her coffee, she filled her mug back up and walked back to Conrad's office and found Abigail, Betty and Martha still huddled together in a secret conference. "Well, ladies," she said, "for now I'm afraid I'm going to have to place...all three of you..." Sarah paused. Three pairs of eyes looked up at her, wide and innocent and elderly and fragile. Arrest was such an ugly, hurtful, scary word. She wanted to use kid gloves and avoid causing the three sisters any unneeded stress. "Uh, what I mean to say is...you're going to have to stay overnight at the station in a...holding cell."

"Oh, just like Perry Mason," Abigail told her sisters in an excited voice. "We're going to sleep in a room with bars."

"Locked up in the Big House," Martha giggled.

"Martha," Betty exclaimed, "where did you learn such language?"

Martha blushed. "I heard a man in a Perry Mason episode say that."

Abigail patted Martha's hand. "Goodness, dear. Leave the prison slang to the hardened criminals."

Sarah felt a smile touch her lips. Sure, she was a little aggravated, but she had to admit the three sisters were a kick. "Uh, ladies, while I'm waiting for Dr. Milton to arrive, do you mind if I ask you a question?"

"We want to remain—" Abigail began to remind Sarah.

"Oh, the question I have isn't about Mitchel Cochran," Sarah promised. She eased over to the desk and sat down on the edge. "I was told that your family once had a feud with Mitchel Cochran's family. Is that true?"

Abigail glanced at her sisters. Betty and Martha quickly placed their hands together and looked forward. Their faces became very stern and upset. "We don't talk about family matters with strangers," Betty told Sarah.

"Indeed, we do not," Martha added in a strict voice.

Abigail nodded. "That thieving Cochran clan…the less said the better. All I will say is that outsiders are not welcome to interfere."

Sarah bit down on her lip and tried to spot some wiggle room. "Ladies, Mitchel Cochran is dead, and your family was feuding with his family. A jury might find that very interesting."

"A jury?" Abigail asked. "What do you mean?"

"Think about it," Sarah said and regretfully added a little pressure. "You ladies admitted to killing a man, so you might have to stand trial before a jury of your peers in a court of law.

Don't you think a jury would find a family feud to be a motive for murder?"

"Oh, just like on Perry Mason," Abigail said and clapped her hands together.

Betty and Martha glanced at each other, lost their stern expressions, and smiled. "This is just like television," they exclaimed.

"No, it's not," Sarah tried to assure the three sisters. "Ladies, this isn't a television show. This is real life. A man is dead and you're going to..." Sarah sighed. "Let's see what Dr. Milton finds, okay? Now, I would love to hear about the feud—"

"We don't talk about that," Betty interrupted her. "Besides, it was long ago…"

Sarah held up her right hand. "I understand," she promised. "All I want to know is if Mitchel Cochran is the last living family member on the Cochran side. Do you know that much? You ladies may be the keepers of some important town history," she said, trying to compliment them. "If he's not the last living Cochran, does he have any children? I'm going to run him through the system in a bit and find out anyway, but you ladies can save me some time."

Abigail glanced at her sisters. "I suppose it wouldn't hurt to tell this nice lady that Mitchel was the last fox in the henhouse."

"I suppose not," Betty and Martha agreed, their worry written plainly on their faces.

Abigail looked at Sarah. "Mitchel Cochran was indeed the last living Cochran," she explained. "He was never married and had no children. He was the last reminder of…what happened."

Sarah nodded. "Thank you," she told Abigail and made a few mental notes. Then the telephone rang. It was Amanda. Dr. Milton had finally arrived. "I have no choice now," Sarah told Amanda when she heard. "Tell Dr. Milton I'll be a few minutes."

"Hurry," Amanda pleaded.

Sarah hung up the phone and looked at Abigail. "I'm afraid I'm going to have to put you three ladies in a cell...for now," she added in a quick voice.

"Sisters," Abigail said excitedly, "let's be brave."

Betty and Martha stood up. "We're ready," they said and marched out of Conrad's office with their wrists crossed in front of them as if expecting genuine handcuffs.

Sarah hesitated and gently grabbed Abigail's arm before she could leave the office. "You have no purses with you. Surely you didn't walk to town?"

"We did," Abigail stated in a proud voice. "The walk is less than half a mile."

Sarah was impressed. The old-timers were certainly tough. "I assumed you must have. I recognized all the trucks that are parked outside."

"My sister Martha drives us when needed. But on a morning like this we decided to walk. We so enjoy our walks in the snow," Abigail explained. "The snow keeps us young."

"I love taking walks in the snow, too," Sarah told Abigail. She felt a kind of friendship between them. Out of the three sisters, Abigail was the most talkative and took the most interest in what Sarah said. "I...wish you could talk about the murder with me. I have so many questions."

"We remain silent, dear," Abigail smiled at Sarah.

"Of course," Sarah sighed. "Uh...do you need me to get

you anything? You might be here a while. Do you or your sisters need medicine or—"

"My sisters and I only take a daily aspirin, a spoonful of cayenne pepper mixed with honey in a snoot of whiskey," Abigail proclaimed. "That and a daily vitamin. We have never been to a doctor and never intend to. Our Papa died when he was a hundred and five and our mother died when she was a hundred and four. My sisters and I have many good years left and don't need some doctor interfering with our health."

"Wow," Sarah said, running her mind back to Los Angeles. She saw herself eating Chinese food and donuts on long stakeouts and dragging her feet for her yearly doctor exams. Suddenly she felt very unhealthy.

"Proper sleep, plenty of walking, and beans," Abigail told Sarah and patted her arm. "Cayenne pepper and honey and whiskey helps the body, too. But the one thing that keeps a person alive is the heart, dear. When the heart grows old, so does the body. When the heart stays young, so does the body." Abigail smiled and patted Sarah's arm again. "Love is the key ingredient."

Sarah stared into Abigail's eyes and saw a beautiful, wise woman who had much wisdom to give. She wanted to hug the woman but instead looked down at her hands. "Sometimes I'm afraid I'll lose the love I have," she said.

"I know," Abigail told Sarah and gently lifted her chin. "Dear, I can read your eyes like I can read the sky. I see goodness in you...but much fear, I'm afraid." Abigail softly let go of Sarah's chin. "You're very afraid to love and be loved except by a rare few that you trust. But the one that you're scared of the most is your husband, am I right? You're afraid he might stop loving you."

"How do you know that?" Sarah begged.

"Because I'm a woman and I was married once, too, dear," Abigail explained with a gentle chuckle. "My husband and I were married for fifty-five years before he wandered off into the woods and met up with a very angry bear."

"I'm so sorry," Sarah told Abigail. "I didn't mean—"

Abigail touched Sarah's arm. "Dear, my husband was a very hard man to love. He had a lot of goodness in him that he rarely showed. He spent his time with the land and not people. He understood animals more than he understood his own children. That's just the way he was, and I accepted that. When he was killed, I let him go. That's what a wife does. But," Abigail said with a gentle smile, "the heart never forgets the love that was once shared."

Sarah felt a tear fall from her eye. "My first husband...betrayed me. I'm remarried now to a good man...I'm so afraid to lose him."

"I know," Abigail promised Sarah and gently hugged her. "Don't be afraid to express your fears to the people you love the most, because the love they have for you is a healing light," she whispered and walked out of the office to join her sisters in the hall.

Sarah watched Abigail leave the office, wiped at her tears, and then drew in a deep breath. "I can't put them in a holding cell," she whispered in a pained voice, "and they don't deserve to be treated like common criminals...but what choice do I have?" And then Sarah suddenly realized she did have a second choice. "This is Snow Falls, after all, and not Los Angeles." She hurried out into the hallway. "Ladies," she said, "what I'm about to propose is against the rules, but I feel that in this case the rules can be broken."

"Broken, dear?" Abigail asked.

"Yes," Sarah explained. "Instead of keeping you here at the station, I want the three of you to go home and promise me you'll stay there. Consider it...a house arrest."

"House arrest?" Betty asked in confusion.

"Yes," Sarah replied gently. "You can't leave your house... cabin...until I say so. I'll have more questions for you. You may miss your walks, but doesn't that sound better than sitting in a drafty old cell with bars?"

Abigail looked at her sisters. "I suppose we're being offered a kindness," she said. "Papa always taught us to never look a gift horse in the mouth."

"And it is getting near lunch," Martha added.

"Indeed it is," Betty agreed and looked at Sarah. "You're a very kind woman. We'll accept your offer."

"Thank you," Sarah replied in a relieved voice. "Now, I'll go get my truck."

"We walked into town and we'll walk home," Abigail told Sarah and held her chin high. "Sisters, let's go home." Betty and Martha stuck their chins up into the air and followed their sister out into the storm, tugging their hats down on their heads and their coats flapping again in the wind. Sarah smiled from ear to ear. The three sisters, she thought, were amazing—and hopefully, she thought to herself, innocent of murder.

Chapter Five

Sarah walked into her coffee shop, shook snow off her hat, coat and boots, and then walked over to a very tall and very thin man standing next to Mitch Cochran's body. "Dr. Milton, thank you for coming," she said.

Dr. Milton looked up with weary eyes. He was a kind man but very stern by nature. At the age of fifty-nine he had become the type of man who spoke very little, tended to his patients, wife and cabin with care, and minded his own business. However, minding his own business was difficult when Sarah was present. The woman had a knack for luring trouble into her path. "Did I really have a choice?" he asked.

"No, I guess you didn't," Sarah replied, spotting Amanda walking out of the kitchen carrying a cup of coffee. Amanda shot her a *he's-in-a-mood* look. Sarah winked at her.

"Here is your coffee."

He did not even look at the body at the table. Dr. Milton removed a heavy gray coat, tossed it down onto a nearby table, stomped more snow off his brown boots, took his coffee from Amanda, and looked at Sarah. "You girls are due to have your blood drawn tomorrow. How are you feeling? Not that I should ask, because you always give the same response."

"Dr. Milton, I feel fine," Sarah promised. "I honestly believe the hot springs burned that awful virus out of our systems."

"Do you?" Dr. Milton asked in a sour voice. "Are you a doctor now, Mrs. Spencer?"

Being called Mrs. Spencer made Sarah feel warm inside. "I'm not a doctor, no. But I know my body."

"Me, too," Amanda carefully eased in. "Our blood tests always show that we're fine and very healthy."

Dr. Milton took a quick sip of coffee. "Too strong," he complained.

Amanda rolled her eyes. "We always brew a strong cup here," she replied with patience.

Sarah stared at Dr. Milton. The man reminded her of a backwoods Jimmy Stewart, hardened yet handsome in an aged kind of way. "Dr. Milton, we need to focus on Mitchel Cochran."

Dr. Milton sighed. "Mr. Cochran isn't going anywhere. Andrew told me that he put you in charge. The man should have his head examined... However, I reckon your reputation as a detective is...known." Dr. Milton peered at her over the rim of his cup as he took another sip of coffee. He cleared his throat, business-like. "I examined the body. I see no signs of physical injury. In my medical opinion, he died of a massive heart attack or an aneurysm. Only the autopsy will tell. But there's no external indications of assault."

Sarah looked over to Amanda, curious about what had transpired before her arrival. Amanda shrugged her shoulders. "I didn't say a word to him, Los Angeles."

Sarah nodded. Dr. Milton knew nothing about the O'Healey sisters' involvement yet. "I saw the ambulance parked outside."

"Need to haul the body to the hospital, Mrs. Spencer. Would have brought my truck but the wife had to keep it to run chores. Ambulance will work fine." He seemed uncomfortable at having to speak so many words about the matter and began edging close to his jacket, eager to head out into the cold as soon as possible and get on with his work.

Sarah lowered her eyes down to the body. "Dr. Milton...please don't think I'm being too pushy, but I'm going to need—"

"An autopsy performed as soon as possible. Yes, Mrs. Spencer, I realize that," Dr. Milton snapped and fought with his scalding hot coffee as he set it down on the table with force. "If it isn't a silly man falling off his roof and breaking his leg—" Dr. Milton glanced at Amanda in order to remind the woman that her own husband had enacted the same catastrophe, "it's a dead man in a coffee shop. I moved to Snow Falls to rest, not be bothered all the time."

"Dr. Milton—" Sarah began to speak.

"And you," Dr. Milton told Sarah, "all you've done is bring trouble to this poor town—" Dr. Milton realized he had spoken more words in a matter of moments than he usually did in an entire month. He looked down at his coffee and shook his head. "Please forgive me...I'm feeling very poorly this morning, myself. My wife and I found out that our son has made...some very bad investments and now says he will have to file for bankruptcy unless I loan him the money he needs to secure his debts."

"I'm very sorry to hear that," Sarah said to Dr. Milton and

then dared to add: "I have…plenty of money. I would be more than happy to help. I may be a newcomer here, but I care about the people of Snow Falls. Always have, always will."

Dr. Milton looked up into Sarah's caring eyes. Guilt and pain struck his heart. "I'm sorry I was so rude, Mrs. Spencer. I was out of line. While it may be true trouble follows you like a shadow under a dog's tail at high noon, that doesn't change the fact that you are a decent woman and a good citizen. Your offer to help a man in need humbles me. I should not have spoken so hastily."

"Then you will accept my offer?"

"No," Dr. Milton shook his head. "In truth, I must allow my son to file for bankruptcy and face the consequences of his bad decisions. That is the most difficult part about being a parent…helping your children mature even when they are already in their thirties. Now, let's focus on Mr. Cochran, shall we?"

"Okay," Sarah agreed. "I believe Mr. Cochran might have been…poisoned."

Dr. Milton drew in a deep breath. "Dare I ask why?" he ventured.

"Love, you better tell Dr. Milton about those three crazy old bats," Amanda told Sarah.

Sarah agreed and carefully explained to Dr. Milton all about Abigail, Betty and Martha O'Healey. When she finished, Dr. Milton looked at her as if she was insane. "Are you out of your mind?" he asked Sarah. "I've known the O'Healey family for a very long time. Those three women wouldn't harm a pantry moth."

"Dr. Milton, they all three admitted to killing Mitchel Cochran," Sarah explained, her voice growing stern. "I don't know how they killed him, though. Or if they are simply talking nonsense in their old age. I'm hoping the autopsy report will help shed some light on this very confusing situation."

Dr. Milton glanced at Amanda. "Do you believe this?" he asked.

"I did hear those women confess to killing Mitchel," Amanda told Dr. Milton. She glanced at the body, shivered all over, and then eased back toward the kitchen. "I'll go pour us some coffee, love," she told Sarah and hurried away.

Dr. Milton lifted his hand and rubbed the back of his neck. "I suppose it could be possible. I always knew there was some bad blood between the Greenlight-O'Healey and Cochran families...but murder? Why, the O'Healey sisters are as harmless as butterflies. This is utter nonsense."

"We have a confession," Sarah reminded Dr. Milton. "I agree that it is strange. We'll need a psychologist to examine them eventually, though it will have to wait until after the storm. After spending a few minutes with the O'Healey sisters I realized they're as harmless as you're claiming, Dr. Milton. But they're also not telling me everything. And the fact remains that they confessed to killing Mr. Cochran."

"And I suppose you have them locked up at the police station?" Dr. Milton asked Sarah in an upset voice.

"No," Sarah sighed. "I didn't...have the heart, okay? I sent them home under house arrest and ordered them to stay there. No more walks into town."

"Well, at least there's that," Dr. Milton replied in a grateful voice.

"Dr. Milton, what do you know about the O'Healey sisters?" Sarah asked.

Dr. Milton took a quick sip of his coffee and then studied Sarah's eyes. "You want information from me?"

"Please. It might help."

Dr. Milton hesitated and then cleared his throat. "It would be nice to warm up with some coffee before I bag up our poor Mr. Cochran. Okay, then. I'll tell you what I know."

"I would be very grateful." Sarah gestured to a chair. Dr. Milton walked over, and they sat down a couple tables over from where the body lay still and limp. Sarah leaned forward toward the doctor. "I want to help the O'Healey sisters, Dr. Milton, not harm them. Anything you can tell me would be very helpful to this case. I can pass your information along to the police psychologist."

"I suppose you do want to help," Dr. Milton said, reading the sincerity in Sarah's eyes. He took another sip of coffee and set down the coffee cup. "I don't usually speak about people. Frustration and anger can make a man speak more words than he's prepared to defend...and I don't like to gossip. But if it will help..."

Sarah leaned back and folded her hands in her lap, relaxing. "Take your time."

"If that man was poisoned," Dr. Milton told Sarah, "time will not be our friend."

"I understand."

Dr. Milton nodded. "Mrs. Spencer—"

"Sarah...please, my name is Sarah."

"I'm a little old fashioned about names," Dr. Milton said with a dry chuckle, then continued. "I've known the O'Healey sisters for many years. However, not as a doctor but as a friend. The O'Healey sisters refuse to see doctors...I doubt any of them have ever seen a doctor, not since their baby vaccinations. On occasion I have struck up conversation with them around town, simply to be friendly, and then perhaps once in a while over the years I have asked a friendly question or two about their diet, tried to figure out if they were experiencing any worrisome symptoms. I've even slipped in little hints like taking baby aspirin as a blood thinner. Strictly as a friend, you understand."

Sarah nodded, impressed. "What about the trouble between the Greenlight and Cochran families?"

Dr. Milton warmed his hands around his coffee mug, thinking back. "All I know is what Abigail told me, years ago, after Mitchel Cochran moved to Snow Falls. You see," Dr. Milton explained, "years ago when this town was nothing but a few cabins and a general store, both the Greenlights and the Cochrans had gold claims here. This was after Matthew Greenlight had been feuding with Billy Cochran over a gold claim somewhere in the Yukon."

"Why did both families move to this area?" Sarah asked, confused.

"Because Miren Cochran married Stephen Greenlight," Dr. Milton explained. "The families were connected through marriage." Dr. Milton finished off his coffee. "Abigail told me that Billy and Meredith Cochran were both very protective over their daughter and vowed to follow her wherever she moved. According to Abigail, when Miren agreed to marry Stephen Greenlight, she only agreed once he accepted the condition that her parents would move with them. In the old days it was not uncommon, living with parents and adult children all in the same home, especially in the frontier era. You had to work together to survive."

Sarah rubbed the tip of her nose and thought for a few

seconds. "Abigail said that Matthew Greenlight claimed Billy Cochran stole gold from his claim. Is that true?"

"From what Abigail claims," Dr. Milton nodded. "Abigail said shortly after the marriage of Miren and Stephen, a feud broke out between the two families, and Stephen Greenlight was forced to leave the Yukon Territory and ended up in this area. He bought a gold claim and, as I explained, so did Billy Cochran. They had fought in the Yukon, but from the way Abigail tells it, there was some thought that a fresh start in a new town would help the families let go of the old enmities." Dr. Milton glanced at the café door as if expecting the sisters to walk in and chide him for telling their secrets. "However, Stephen had a distaste for Billy Cochran, and moving to a new town couldn't wipe that out. They only ever tolerated each other because Stephen loved Billy's daughter. As Abigail tells the story, the day came when Stephen publicly claimed Billy Cochran stole from his claim—dug up a sack of gold nuggets already mined, one that only Miren knew the location of. He claimed Billy had bullied his own daughter into revealing the location of the hidden gold, then stolen it in retribution for the old feud between the families. Abigail said Stephen wrote in a letter that was intercepted that he had had enough and threatened to kill Billy Cochran. Some kind of a duel. Pistols at high noon, Alaska style."

"How did Stephen Greenlight's wife respond?"

"According to Abigail," Dr. Milton continued, "Miren Cochran left her husband, fled to a cousin's house amid the trouble. Stephen Greenlight, infuriated, believed her departure was proof that her own father had hurt her, so Stephen swore he would never rest until Billy Cochran and his entire family were...dead." Dr. Milton looked at the door again and leaned forward. "As it turns out, Billy refused to meet Stephen for a pistol fight, said it was a slur on his honor to even respond. That very day, Abigail said, Stephen Greenlight drew a line on his property and threatened to kill any Cochran who dared to step over it. Billy Cochran drew a line and dared any Greenlight to step over it. Thus, the feud, one that began in the Yukon Territory, became renewed right here in Snow Falls."

"And then some," Sarah added, stunned. It was worse than she thought.

Amanda appeared, carrying a fresh pot of coffee and two empty coffee mugs. "More coffee, Dr. Milton?" she dared to ask.

"Please."

Amanda shot a surprised look at Sarah. "Your coffee must be rubbing off on him."

"Guess so," Sarah agreed and took one of the empty mugs from Amanda.

"Here you go," Amanda said and carefully refilled Dr. Milton's mug and then Sarah's. "Mind if I join you?"

"Not at all," Sarah assured Amanda.

Amanda sat down, filled her own mug full of coffee, placed the pot of coffee down on the table, and looked at Dr. Milton. "I've been listening from the kitchen," she confessed. "And I have a question."

"Okay," Dr. Milton said, as he shifted in his chair.

"If the O'Healey sisters and Mitchel Cochran are all still living in Snow Falls, that must mean there is a reason, right? Like maybe...gold...or some other hidden treasure?" Amanda asked. "I mean, let's face it, Snow Falls isn't exactly the tropics. Yet the sisters come back here all the time."

Dr. Milton took a sip of his coffee. "I've often wondered why the O'Healey sisters travel back to Snow Falls each winter," he confessed. "Actually, Mitchel Cochran leaves Snow Falls in the spring and returns when winter arrives, too. He visits his two daughters who both live in Los Angeles." Dr. Milton lowered his coffee. "I wish I had an answer, but I do not. Abigail only spoke to me about the feud because my wife is a very close friend who Abigail, Betty and Martha all love. As a matter of fact," Dr. Milton said in a serious voice, "it was my wife who asked Abigail about the feud. I, like yourself," he told Amanda, "simply listened and asked a few curious questions here and there. Abigail only answered because my wife was curious too, and now that I think about it...Betty and Martha didn't seem very happy about us learning all these details...or that Abigail was even allowing it."

Sarah took a sip of coffee. The coffee was perfect in her view. "Dr. Milton, the O'Healey sisters have many children, from what they told me. I need to run a check on each family member. I'll also run Mr. Cochran through the system and start checking on his family. It may be someone other than the O'Healey sisters who killed Mr. Cochran—"

"Utter nonsense," Dr. Milton told Sarah.

"I have to check under every bed, Dr. Milton, and sweep out the dust bunnies," Sarah explained. "That's my job. Your job is to perform an autopsy."

"I know my job, Mrs. Spencer."

"Then let's work as a team and solve this case together, Dr. Milton." Sarah put down her coffee. "It's possible that the O'Healey sisters killed Mr. Cochran...somehow. Maybe with a poison? But I don't see how...not yet. I suppose we should search their house. It's also possible an outsider killed him, perhaps with a long-acting poison that took effect only this morning. The O'Healey sisters did claim they killed Mr. Cochran without touching him. But," Sarah said in a very careful voice, "the O'Healey sisters can say one thing and mean another. They're old and the wordage they use can be a bit enigmatic. I want to be very careful before jumping to conclusions. I want solid data backed up by concrete facts and evidence. The lives of three women are on the line here and before I'm prepared to mark them as guilty, I want to dig under the snow and locate the truth."

Dr. Milton respected Sarah's concern and professionalism. "Okay, Mrs. Spencer, we will work as a team," he assured Sarah. "I care about the O'Healeys myself. Besides, ever since I began taking cayenne and honey together every night before bed, my health has improved. I owe them a debt of gratitude."

"Cayenne pepper and honey?" Amanda asked, confused.

"Don't ask...not yet anyway," Sarah told Amanda and patted her arm. "Drink your coffee, because after Dr. Milton leaves with the body, we're locking up and going back to the station to put our noses to the grindstone."

Amanda sighed. "So much for girls-only week," she said and looked at Mitchel Cochran's still form slumped over the table and the forgotten newspaper. "Of all mornings...thanks a heap," she grumbled.

The doctor shot her a strange look. "What was that?"

"Uh, I said, rest in peace," Amanda quickly added, guilt passing over her face as she gulped down the last of her coffee.

Chapter Six

Amanda paced around Conrad's office like a tiger anxious to escape from a cage. "Our entire day is being wasted because a few old bats killed a cranky old man. Or want us to think they did."

Sarah lowered a report she was studying. "It says here," she said, bypassing Amanda's complaints, "that Mitchel Cochran has two daughters."

"We know that," Amanda pointed out. She walked over to a chair, grabbed a cup full of hot cocoa off Conrad's desk, and plopped down. "Did we really need to have a computer tell us something that we already know?"

"No," Sarah replied. "But this report goes into a lot of detail." Sarah grabbed a half-eaten cheeseburger Amanda had trekked down to the diner and purchased for their lunch. The scent of french fries and melting cheese lingered in the chilly air of the station. "Mitchel Cochran's two daughters have both been arrested for real estate fraud. His oldest daughter was released from prison five months ago and his youngest daughter was released eight months ago, three months earlier than her sister, for good behavior."

"Real estate fraud?" Amanda asked.

Sarah nodded, scanning down the police report details. "They were buying bad properties and then obtaining false appraisals to raise the price of the property in order to sell it and make a profit. Mostly they bought old buildings under a shell company called Ceiling Properties, had the buildings appraised by a dishonest appraiser, and then sold them to companies as rental properties."

"Are these two women married?" Amanda said, her brow furrowed in thought.

"Both are divorced, no children...no other siblings," Sarah explained and took a bite of her cheeseburger. The cheese dripped out on her finger and she licked it up, glad for the filling meal with such an investigation before them. "I wonder if Mr. Cochran knew?" she asked and quickly wiped a bit of ketchup off the side of her mouth with a crumpled brown napkin.

Amanda rubbed her chin. She remained cranky about the turn of events in her day but what was the point of fussing? The least she could do for Sarah was focus on the case at hand. Complaining wouldn't make the day go by any faster. "I knew Mitchel Cochran was a cantankerous old man...but I never knew he was a bad guy."

Sarah took another bite of her cheeseburger. "We don't really know the truth of those old claims of thieving, let's remember. What we do know is that both the O'Healey sisters and Mr. Cochran leave Snow Falls to visit their children when winter ends," she said. "It's obvious the O'Healey sisters and

Mr. Cochran have reason to harbor lingering harsh feelings toward one another…"

"But?" Amanda asked, reading Sarah's doubts.

"It's strange how they all leave town when winter ends," Sarah mused.

"Are you implying those three old bats and that cranky old man are somehow connected in…a bad scheme of some sort?" Amanda asked.

"No…nothing like that," Sarah explained. "I'm wondering if Mr. Cochran was somehow following the O'Healey sisters. If his own daughters are criminals…" Sarah looked out the office window and listened as the storm howled particularly loud for a second. "I want to examine Mr. Cochran's cabin and see how he lived. I need to see who he really was."

"Well…one of us is supposed to stay here at all times, but I would rather go with you," Amanda told Sarah. "I don't like being alone."

"The only person who has called today has been Conrad and Andrew," Sarah said and polished off the rest of her cheeseburger. "It's almost two o'clock and the phone has been silent. I'm sure we can leave for a while without Snow Falls crumbling down to the ground. And if someone does call, they can leave a message. Besides, everyone in town knows Andrew's home phone number, if they don't reach someone here, they'll just call him directly."

"Good thing Andrew can't hear you say that. He'll put you in charge of a new 911 call center," Amanda teased.

Sarah smiled. "I can't stand sitting behind a desk. Pete is the same way and I learned under him. We like to work our legs."

"Hey, maybe we should call Pete for help," Amanda suggested.

"I thought of that, but honestly, June Bug, the poor guy is exhausted. I think I'll leave him alone for a while," Sarah explained and grabbed a cup of coffee. "Now, the next report I ran is on all of the O'Healey children."

"Anything good?" Amanda asked and sipped her hot cocoa.

"Clean as a whistle," Sarah shrugged. "Every son or daughter of the O'Healey sisters works a very respectable job. One guy works as a medical researcher. Nothing more than parking tickets on their records."

"Maybe the researcher is the one who suggested taking cayenne pepper and honey?" Amanda suggested.

"Could be," Sarah rubbed her chin and continued. "All of the O'Healey children are married to people who have never broken the law. All of the grandchildren attend private Christian schools. As far as I can tell we're looking at an all-American, crime-free family."

"So that leaves us with the two bad sisters on the Greenlight side who like to make easy money."

Sarah grabbed a pencil and piece of notepaper and wrote something down. "A reminder for when I get back."

"A reminder for what?"

"I need to call the prison Mr. Cochran's daughters were housed in and see if he ever visited them, and if he did, when and what times."

"Good thinking," Amanda told Sarah, even though she wasn't sure what path Sarah's mind was walking down. Her brow wrinkled as she thought about it further, however. "Los Angeles, the old man is dead. I don't see how calling a prison and finding out if he visited his daughters will help us solve his murder."

"I'm not sure myself...yet," Sarah confessed. "I just need to know if there was some kind of pattern that might help us. More importantly, I'm still trying to understand the O'Healey sisters. They admitted to killing Mr. Cochran but said they didn't touch him. What does that mean?"

"Maybe they scared him to death?" Amanda suggested and drained her hot cocoa and then wiped her mouth with the arm of her dress. "So good."

Sarah leaned back in Conrad's chair and began nibbling her lip. "If they didn't use poison...then how?" she asked. "They also said they waited too long to kill him. That makes it clear to me that they were planning to kill him before today."

"Or that they're just plain crazy. I can just imagine those three old bats sitting around, sipping tea, eating custard tarts, and planning a murder," Amanda said and rolled her eyes. "Oh, let's stab him...oh no, we must shoot him...oh goodness no, we must hit him in the head with a pipe," she continued in a silly old woman's voice. "And then we'll drag him outside and bury him under the mums in the flower garden...he'll surely be a delightful fertilizer."

Sarah nearly spit coffee out of her mouth. "June Bug, that's awful," she laughed.

Amanda rolled her eyes again. "With those three old bats anything is possible," she told Sarah, leaning forward to snatch a few salty fries out of her friend's to-go container and gobble them down. "They admitted to killing Mitchel Cochran, love. Isn't that enough to throw the book at them? Why all the fuss? Let's lock them up and let the lawyer sort out the mess."

"June Bug, that's illegal, first of all, but most importantly I don't think they're guilty of murder," Sarah explained. "If I did, I would have them locked up right now. I think it's possible...maybe...I could be wrong...that they saw something they didn't understand. Or perhaps they're covering for someone." Sarah put down her coffee. "You did say you heard the front door to the coffee shop open."

"Yes, love, I did," Amanda confirmed. "And when I peeked out into the front room, I saw the O'Healey sisters. My eyes didn't spot another living person. No one was hiding under a table or in the corners, love."

Sarah began nibbling on her lower lip again as her mind struggled against the confusion taunting her. "There has to be a sensible explanation," she insisted.

"Love," Amanda said in a voice that told Sarah she was asking for the impossible, "we've fought against people who are anything but sensible. The psycho model...Mr. Mafia...the crooked FBI agent...and how can we ever forget Ms. Nasty Virus who nearly killed us at the hot springs? And if that wasn't enough, we had a killer come all the way from London to try and kill us. I'm sorry, love, but sensible killers are not on the menu."

"The Back Alley Killer wasn't sensible either," Sarah admitted. "But each killer has a reason...and in their minds that reason was sensible. That's what I'm trying to imply, June Bug. The O'Healey sisters obviously wanted Mr. Cochran dead, but look at their age. They could have killed Mr. Cochran when they were younger, stronger, with their minds sharper and intact. Why wait this late in the game?"

Amanda considered Sarah's question. "Maybe they wanted to make Mitchel sweat it out?"

Sarah shrugged her shoulders. "I don't know. All I do

know is that I have a few facts and a bag full of questions that need to be answered." Sarah checked the clock hanging on the office wall. "It'll be dark soon. We need to go."

Amanda sighed. "I'll get our coats," she said, then asked, "I guess there's no chance that we can make a side stop at O'Mally's and do a little shopping, is there?"

"I wish we could," Sarah replied in a sad voice. "I doubt O'Mally's is even open in this storm. I wish Conrad were home handling this case and we were at O'Mally's, walking down our favorite aisle, browsing through the beautiful clothes—"

"Having the time of our lives."

"And then resting in the snack bar," Sarah agreed, "for a cappuccino and a freshly baked cookie."

Amanda sighed again. "Love, I'm about ready to cry."

"Me, too," Sarah moaned. "The truth is, June Bug, I know I have work to do as a cop, but deep down I want to shop until I drop, drive back to my cabin, bake a cake, start a fire, and play in the snow."

"I know what you mean," Amanda replied. "Civic duty isn't all it's cracked up to be. Speaking of cabins, it's a good thing you had Conrad put in a doggy door for Mittens. At least she's at home all nice and warm and happy and can let herself out to tinkle if she needs to."

"She's very spoiled," Sarah pointed out, and a fond smirk crossed her lips.

"I wouldn't mind being spoiled myself."

Sarah forced a cheerful smile to her face. "I promise to take you shopping when this case is solved, June Bug."

"You better," Amanda smiled back.

"You have my—" Sarah began to reply but was interrupted by the phone. "I better get that."

"I'll go get our coats," Amanda said, grabbed a few more fries, and left the office.

Sarah grabbed the phone. "Hello, Detective Gar...Spencer speaking. How may I help you?"

"Mrs. Spencer, this is Dr. Milton," Dr. Milton greeted Sarah in a serious tone of voice.

"Dr. Milton, is everything okay?"

"I drew blood from Mr. Cochran and sent it to the lab while I prepared the autopsy," Dr. Milton explained. "On your suggestion of the possibility of poisons, I ran a series of specialized blood, tissue, and hair follicle tests."

"You performed the autopsy already?" Sarah asked, surprised.

"Not yet," Dr. Milton explained. "Sarah, there are rules I have to follow and people I have to call. I can't perform an autopsy until I get a green light."

"Right, right. I'm aware of the rules, Dr. Milton."

"Good," Dr. Milton told Sarah. He cleared his throat uncomfortably. "Rules are very important to follow. However, there aren't any rules against drawing a few tubes of blood and other samples. Well, there are...but what certain people don't know won't hurt them. No one is going to miss a little blood."

Sarah felt a deep respect for Dr. Milton. The man could be strict and even difficult at times, but he knew when to bend the rules in order to discover the truth. "Dr. Milton, what did the tests reveal?"

"Poison," Dr. Milton stated. "A very deadly poison in sufficient quantity to stop the heart within seconds of injection."

Sarah closed her eyes in pain. "Any idea how the poison was delivered?"

"Mrs. Spencer," Dr. Milton said, standing in a cramped office full of medical books and old hunting photos, "I found no sign of violence on Mr. Cochran. I searched the man's entire body, in between his toes, his head, behind his ears, his neck, in between his fingers, his belly button, underneath his arms, every nook and cranny you can think of. I found a few old scars, some recent scrapes caused by carrying firewood, and nothing else. The only suggestion I can make is that it wasn't injected."

"What are you saying?" Sarah said in confusion.

"I don't normally make suggestions, but one possibility you should consider is whether the poison was placed in Mr. Cochran's coffee and he drank it."

Sarah saw a hideous snowman chewing a candy cane amidst a powerful storm. The black leather jacket covering the snowman flapped menacingly in the icy winds. *You will never escape, Sarah...I'll always be around to get you...boo...*

Sarah shook the image from her mind. "What's the name of the poison, Dr. Milton? What can you tell me about it?"

"Mr. Cochran's heart enzymes were saturated with the poison," Dr. Milton explained. "The man died of a massive, instant heart attack. As for the name of the poison...I don't know. I'm trying to determine the name now."

Sarah opened her eyes. "Dr. Milton, could the O'Healey sisters have created this poison?"

"Mrs. Spencer...Abigail O'Healey's son is a medical researcher. It's...possible," Dr. Milton confessed in a miserable voice. "I'm afraid...my opinion of the O'Healey sisters might be...biased." Dr. Milton was quiet for a moment. "Please don't let my opinion of my fellow Snow Falls citizens affect you in the performance of your duties, Mrs. Spencer. You have a duty to perform. I expect you to do it."

Sarah felt a deep shot of grief enter her heart. "I wish there was some other way, Dr. Milton. But as it stands, right now I have to allow the evidence to guide my course of action."

"Yes, Mrs. Spencer, you do," Dr. Milton agreed. "I'll be in touch."

Sarah heard Dr. Milton hang up. She put down the phone and turned around. Amanda was standing in the doorway holding her coat. "Those three old bats poisoned Mitchel, didn't they?" she asked.

"Someone poisoned him," Sarah said and took her coat from Amanda. "Right now, all the evidence is pointing at the O'Healey sisters. But we need more proof."

"Are you going to arrest them?" Amanda asked. "I mean, I know they're old and kooky, but it's a little sad to imagine them behind bars."

"I'm not going to arrest them...yet," Sarah promised. "We'll drive out to Mr. Cochran's cabin and look around. Maybe we can find clues that will help us."

"You still think the O'Healey sisters are covering for the real killer, don't you?" Amanda asked.

"June Bug, Mr. Cochran was killed by a very deadly poison. Abigail O'Healey's son is a medical researcher. I'm worried the old woman might be covering for her son...but she's not acting in that way. Instead, all three women seem very excited about the murder." Sarah shook her head. "It doesn't make sense. There's got to be more to the story. Come on, June Bug, and let's hurry. Old Steve is about to make his last plow run of the day and we need to stay ahead of the storm."

Amanda slid on her gloves and tossed on her hat. "Love," she said, "someday I'm going to get through a winter without a murder taking place. And when that happens, I'm going to faint in the snow and have some hunter find my body when spring arrives."

Sarah put on her coat. "June Bug," she replied, "I'll be right next to you. Come on."

Outside in the snow a strange figure lurked, unseen and unheard, footsteps silent in the snowdrifts that piled ever higher along the streets and sidewalks of Snow Falls.

Chapter Seven

Sarah drove her jeep down a snow-packed driveway. The tires on the jeep fought through the snow, crunching across hidden rocks, struggling to find purchase. Large, snow-coated trees loomed over the driveway, with heavy limbs drooping down and threatening to crush the small wooden cabin on its small lot. "I didn't realize Mitchel Cochran lived so far out," Amanda said in a worried voice. "I hope we make it back to town."

"The snow has eased up some," Sarah told Amanda as she eased her jeep to a stop. "I'm sure if we hurry, we'll be able to make it back into town before the snow becomes heavy again."

Amanda looked forward and studied the small cabin. The cabin's roofed porch sagged under the weight of rows of dry, stacked firewood; the left side of the cabin was lined with more firewood in a tidy row and covered with a thick gray tarp, now barely visible with the snowdrifts. As far as Amanda could see, the cabin appeared normal—just like any other rugged cabin in Alaska. "What exactly are you looking for?" she asked.

"I'm not sure," Sarah confessed. She let her jeep stand idle for a couple of minutes and warmed her gloved hands against the vents. "To be honest, June Bug, this case has me baffled. The O'Healey sisters don't seem very upset about Mr. Cochran's death. In fact, they appear excited over being marked as suspects. It's like..." Sarah paused and stared at the snowy cabin. No smoke issued from the chimney. She knew that made sense because a dead man surely could not stoke a fire, yet it still gave the cabin a dark and cold appearance.

"It's like what?" Amanda asked.

"June Bug," Sarah responded in a troubled voice, "it's like the O'Healey sisters actually believe they killed Mr. Cochran in a way that they planned...but I think he was, in fact, killed another way. The only problem with that theory is that you only remember hearing the door to the coffee shop open once...which leads me to believe someone entered the coffee shop with the O'Healey sisters...the real killer. But when I think about that idea too much, that doesn't make sense, either. We're missing some important pieces of information."

"But you're not ruling out the O'Healey sisters being the real killers, right?" Amanda asked in a regretful voice.

"Abigail O'Healey's son is a medical researcher," Sarah sighed. "I'm afraid the O'Healey sisters are in some really hot water now that we know Mr. Cochran died from poison." Sarah turned off her jeep and opened the door. "We better try and stay ahead of the snow."

"I guess we should," Amanda agreed. She opened her own door, eased out into an icy wind, shivered, and carefully walked to the front of the jeep. "The temperature is dropping. All the roads will turn into an ice sheet within a few hours."

Sarah cradled her arms together. "We need to use caution,"

she stated over the howling winds. "I'm sure no one is in the cabin. The snow isn't disturbed, and it looks like no one has been here, but you can never tell."

Amanda nodded. "You have your gun, right?"

Sarah glanced down at her ankle. Her holster rested just inside the lining of her snow boots. "Yeah," she said, "but I don't want to pull it out...not yet anyway. If someone is watching us, I don't want them knowing I have a gun."

Amanda studied the cabin. As she did, a powerful gust of wind swept through the trees and shocked the snow right off the evergreen limbs above them. A pile of snow dropped right down onto Amanda's head. "Oh..." Amanda shouted and began slapping snow off her face, "could this day get any worse?"

Sarah fought back a grin. "Come on, June Bug," she said and began fighting her way through the snow toward the front porch of the cabin. The snow quickly began to make war with the boots on her feet, allowing the cold to slip through and transform her feet into frozen blocks of ice. No matter how warm a fortress a person's clothing was in Alaska, Sarah thought, the cold always found a way into the castle.

"I'm coming...I'm coming," Amanda fussed and hurried after Sarah, lumbering through the high drifts like a frozen bear emerging from an iceberg. Even though she absolutely adored the snow and loved the cold, the stormy day wasn't appearing to make her a fan. "No shopping...no girls' week...no nothing except being cold and confused," she mumbled under her breath. "Being a cop stinks."

Sarah heard Amanda grumbling to herself but didn't say anything. She understood her best friend's frustration. After all they had been through together it was a shame to be stuck inside another murder case that resisted their investigation. "Steps are slippery...careful," Sarah called out as she navigated the front porch.

"I'll be careful, love," Amanda promised. "I wouldn't want Dr. Milton fussing at me for breaking a leg, now would I? I mean, that bloke would love it if everyone lived inside of a protective bubble in order to spare him the inconvenience of actually having to perform his medical duties, right?"

Sarah shook her head and grinned and held out a hand to help her best friend up the last couple steps safely. At the top of the steps, Sarah reached into her right pocket, pulled out the set of keys she had found in Mitchel Cochran's coat pocket, and then looked to her left and right. The front porch was freezing cold, nothing but snow drifts and icy winds— winds that swirled the snow around at their feet but didn't disturb the accumulated snow too much. "No tracks," she said. "No one has been on the front porch."

Amanda stepped up beside Sarah. "Let's hurry inside," she begged. "My ears are freezing off."

Sarah studied the front porch for a few more seconds, soaking in as much detail as her mind would allow her to absorb, and then hurried to the sturdy wooden front door and disengaged the door lock with a silver key. "Okay," she said, "I'll go in first. You stand right here until it's safe and I call for you. Okay?"

"Love, we're a team," Amanda reminded Sarah. "I'm not letting you go inside alone."

Sarah looked into Amanda's caring face. "Let's go," she smiled. She carefully eased the front door open and stepped into a small living room. Amanda followed closely behind. "Careful," Sarah whispered. "Close the door."

Amanda nodded, pushed the front door closed, and then looked around the living room. The first thing she noticed was a stone fireplace that had soft red coals glowing in it. The coals were dark red and quickly dying out. "Mitchel left a fire going when he drove into town," Amanda whispered.

Sarah locked her eyes on the fireplace. "It seems that way," she agreed and then turned her attention to the rest of the living room. She spotted a bookshelf with neatly shelved books, a clean but old brown recliner, and a couch grouped around a coffee table with an old brass lamp. A few photos of the northern wilderness hung on the log walls. "Very basic," she whispered and then turned her attention to a small kitchen only separated from the living room by a simple wooden dining table with a few chairs. The kitchen too appeared clean, organized and unremarkable. Sarah checked a few drawers and cupboards but found nothing special or out of the ordinary. "Let's explore down that hallway."

Amanda followed Sarah. They found two doors. One door opened into a small bathroom that was neat and clean. The second door led into a spartan bedroom that held a bed, a reading chair with a lamp, a night stand, and a closet only partly full of clothes, mostly the typical plaid flannel shirts and wool sweaters he preferred. "Mitchel wasn't a very materialistic person, was he?" Amanda asked, noting the half-empty closet and the lack of decoration. "No woman's touch here."

Sarah walked over to the reading chair and looked down at a small table next to it. She spotted a tobacco pipe carefully resting across an old black lacquer ashtray. "I guess not," she said and picked up the pipe and smelled it. "Cheap cherry tobacco."

"Cheap everything," Amanda pointed out. "All of this furniture looks like it could have come from a thrift store."

Sarah put the pipe back down and walked over to the brown plaid curtain that looked worn and almost threadbare in a few places. She ran her hands across the curtains, thought for a second, and then turned to Amanda. "No photos of any family members," she mused.

"Not a one," Amanda said.

"If Mr. Cochran doesn't have any photos of his daughters...that makes me wonder if he was close to them. I didn't find any photos of his two daughters in the wallet I found on his body, either."

Amanda walked over to the man's twin-sized bed and examined an old graying quilt. At one time it might have been a dull blue color, but it had faded with too many washings and lacked all color now. "Feels like a dungeon in here. Very dreary."

Sarah studied the open closet door. "I want to examine the closet a little closer."

"Okay, love." Amanda smoothed her hand over the quilt again with a sad expression and watched as Sarah got to work.

Sarah walked over to the closet door, peeked her head inside, and found a light. She switched it on and began to examine the clothes, worn-down boots, and a box full of winter hats and work gloves. Nothing looked like it had been bought in the last ten or twenty years. No other items were present on the shelves or in the back of the closet, no matter how many times she looked. "Clean," she said in a disappointed voice.

"Let's go back to the living room," Amanda suggested.

Sarah closed the closet door. "Let me look under the bed

first," she said and knelt down for a quick look, not expecting to find anything more than dust bunnies. To her shock, she spotted a small wooden box. "Found something," she called out and retrieved the box and placed it on the bed.

"A box?" Amanda asked. "Hmm...this could be interesting."

Sarah studied the latch and found it secured by a lock. "Wonder if any of the keys I found in Mr. Cochran's coat will work?" she asked and began to examine the keys. Amanda watched, anxious to find out what secrets might be inside. When Sarah came up short, Amanda sighed. "We'll take the box back to the station," Sarah explained, "and open it there."

"Then let's hurry back to the station."

Sarah picked up the box, walked out of the bedroom, and went back to the kitchen. "June Bug, check the refrigerator for me."

Amanda hurried over to what appeared to be a Westinghouse refrigerator out of the sixties, opened it using the old fashioned latch, and studied the contents. "Bread...bologna...leftovers that look like chili...a few root beer sodas...nothing much. Freezer has an ice tray...and..." She reached in and then hastily dropped something. "A bag of peas that's probably older than I am," Amanda said, making a face as she shut the freezer.

Sarah set the wooden box down on the kitchen table and explored the kitchen cabinets. "One plate, one bowl, one mug, one glass...hardly much in his pantry aside from some canned soup," she called out. "It's clear that Mitchel didn't entertain much company."

Amanda made her way to the bookshelf in the living room

and began going through the books. "All westerns, love," she called out. "Cheap thrift store books."

Sarah bit down on her lower lip. "I found a few dollars in Mr. Cochran's wallet, his driver's license, a bank card and a few coupons for coffee creamer. From what we've seen and found it would appear Mitchel Cochran was one of two things: a very poor man, or a man who didn't like to spend money."

Amanda went to the fireplace and held her hands over the dying coals and had a thought. "Love, there's a great deal of firewood outside that's been hauled in by someone. It's professionally bundled, I saw the zip tie strapping on the porch. That much firewood costs money."

Sarah thought about the firewood outside. "That makes sense. Mr. Cochran couldn't have cut that much firewood by himself."

"I didn't see a work shed outside, either," Amanda added. "No chain saws hanging about and no axe leaning in a corner. He had it delivered. He's just a tightwad."

Sarah walked to the living room window, pulled back a yellowing curtain that was just as raggedy as the curtains in the bedroom, and looked out into the small back yard. It was bare of any work buildings and abutted the tree line after only a few yards; the trees were dense with thicket and she doubted he had any outbuildings in the forest. "Snow is picking up," she said, "we better get back to the station."

"I'm with you, love," Amanda said in a relieved voice. She hurried to the front door and opened it as Sarah grabbed the wooden box. "At least we're not leaving empty-handed."

Sarah handed Amanda the wooden box. "Let's hope not,"

she said and locked the front door. "Be careful going down the front steps, June Bug."

"You bet," Amanda smiled, happy to be going back to town. She carefully navigated her way back to the jeep, fighting her way through the drifts, turning her head against the icy winds, and waited for Sarah. Sarah remained on the front porch for a moment, studying the firewood, and then worked her way out into the snow. "What were you looking at?" Amanda asked as they climbed into the jeep and watched the snow turn heavier by the minute.

"I have my firewood delivered by Mr. Richmond," Sarah explained, brushing off the snow soaking her coat. "Mr. Richmond isn't cheap."

"My hubby buys his firewood from Mr. Richmond, too. The entire town does, I think," Amanda stated. "Mr. Richmond owns over eight hundred acres of timber land from what I was told."

"Nine hundred," Sarah corrected Amanda. "But that's not what I'm focused on. I'm focused on the tarp covering the wood. Mr. Richmond supplies his customers with red tarps. Easier to see in the snow. The tarp on that porch is gray. But also, that much wood..." Sarah looked back at the porch. "June Bug, I'm sure Mr. Richmond would have provided a tarp for Mr. Cochran if he had bought that much wood from him."

"You're probably right," Amanda said in an excited voice. But her excitement quickly turned into a frown. "Los Angeles, I hate to ask this...but so what?"

"I'm not sure," Sarah replied. "But I think it means Mr. Cochran doesn't get his wood delivered from Mr. Richmond." She raised her head and studied the stormy sky. "It's getting darker. We better get back to town," she said and quickly buckled up. "Ready?"

"Ready," Amanda said, holding the wooden box in her lap. "Let's make tracks...uh, careful tracks, love."

Sarah backed her jeep away from the cabin and aimed for town. "I'll turn up the heat."

"That would be wonderful," Amanda smiled. "My ears are about to fall off."

Sarah turned up the heat and focused on the snowy road. "Mr. Cochran drove a run-down truck," she told Amanda. "I had Jacob Bates come and haul the truck to the towing yard for safekeeping since it would be in the way of the plows anyway. I wonder if he'll do me a favor?"

"What kind of favor?" Amanda asked, watching the windshield wipers on the jeep fight snow off the windshield.

"All I found in the cabin of the truck was the truck's registration card, an insurance card, and a tire gauge of the bed of the truck. What I didn't look for was wood."

"You mean firewood?" Amanda asked.

Sarah nodded. "O'Mally sells gray tarps, June Bug," she explained. "I'm wondering if Mr. Cochran did get his wood on his own after all...perhaps from someone that might not be a stranger?"

Amanda looked at Sarah. "Not a stranger?" she asked and then caught on. "Oh, my," she gasped, "you're thinking Mitchel has a relative in Snow Falls, someone other than his two daughters?"

Sarah nodded and didn't say another word until they arrived safely back in town.

Chapter Eight

Sarah slipped behind Conrad's desk and picked up the telephone. "I need to call the O'Healey sisters," she told Amanda.

Amanda set the wooden box down on the desk and removed her coat. "The way the storm is growing no one is going anywhere tonight," she replied, grateful to be back in town. "This station isn't a five-star resort, but it's safe and warm."

Sarah called the O'Healey sisters' home and waited. Abigail picked up on the fourth ring. "Hi, this is Detective Garland...Spencer," Sarah told Abigail. "I was afraid you weren't home for a second."

"When the body gets old, dear," Abigail explained, and when she shifted her stance, Sarah heard the click of fancy high heels against tile floors in the background, "it takes time to walk to the telephone." Since when did these hardy old sisters wear high heels at home?

"I suppose you're right," Sarah agreed. "Anyway, I was

calling to check on you and make sure you were safely at home."

"My sisters and I are dressed in our evening gowns, dear," Abigail chided Sarah. "Once we don our evening gowns, we do not leave home. It's not proper."

"Evening gowns?" Sarah asked and then stuffed her question into the back of her mind. "Oh, well that sounds nice. I'm glad you're all home, safe and sound. The storm eased up for a bit but now it's drawing back with some dangerous power. I want everyone to stay inside."

Abigail made a genteel sound of agreement. "Dear, when one has lived through as many winters as we have, one understands that the night cold is far different from the day cold. The night changes the cold into a deadly creature that grown men fear. You can rest assured that my sisters and I have no intention of leaving our home. Besides, the Perry Mason show will be on the television in less than an hour. Martha is making the popcorn and Betty is preparing the hot cider." Her voice trilled merrily.

Sarah felt a smile touch her lips. In her mind she saw the three sisters huddled around an old television set, sitting on a couch together in dresses that reminded them of their former youthful selves, sharing popcorn and oohing and ahhing as Perry Mason tangled with a criminal. But then her smile faded. A man lay dead—poisoned. She had to solve the murder, even if it meant trampling on the fantasies of three old ladies. "I'll be in touch tomorrow morning, okay?"

"Of course, dear," Abigail smiled. "You're such a nice woman. It's a shame that you can't be trusted."

Sarah sighed. "Abigail, I was only trying to imply that not every cop can be trusted—"

"Now, now, dear, I understand," Abigail interrupted Sarah with a soft voice. "There is no need to explain yourself."

Sarah felt like banging the phone against her head. "Abigail, please listen to me," she pleaded. "I'm not a bad cop. I can be trusted. All I need is for you and your sisters to talk to me—"

"Oh no," Abigail said in a quick voice, "my sisters and I wish to remain silent. You said we have that choice, dear. Remember?"

Amanda gave Sarah a curious look. Sarah rolled her eyes. "I remember, Abigail...I remember," she sighed. "I'll be in touch tomorrow morning to check on you." Sarah quickly decided to take the moment to see if she could get Abigail to talk about her son. If Abigail wasn't willing to talk about the murder then maybe, Sarah thought, she could get the old woman to reveal a few clues without realizing she was doing so. "Abigail, before I go, I need to inform you that I have to contact your children."

Abigail beamed. "Dear, I already have," she said. "I've contacted my three sons and my daughter. They are very pleased to hear that the feud is now ended, and that Mitchel Cochran is dead."

Sarah removed her winter hat and tossed it down on the desk in frustration rather than voice her true thoughts to the woman. She forced a calm smile to her face as she replied, "Abigail, you never told me what your children do for a living. Whatever they do I'm sure you're very proud," she said, hoping to lure Abigail into complacency by complimenting her children. Sarah hated herself for trying to trick an old woman but knew that unless she forced Abigail and her sisters to talk, she wasn't going to get anywhere. At least this was better than arresting them and subjecting them to a real police interrogation.

"Oh yes," Abigail smiled from ear to ear with pride. "My three sons and my daughter are highly educated and respected citizens. I made it my life goal to provide my children with the absolute best. My efforts have been rewarded."

"What do your children do?" Sarah repeated, faking polite interest.

"My Jessica is a pediatric nurse," Abigail told Sarah in a happy voice. "She takes care of babies. My Andy is a stock broker. He does very well for himself."

"I bet."

Abigail smiled and continued. "My Timothy is a college professor. He teaches math. And my sweet, sweet Caleb has made medicine his life and chose to become a medical researcher. Oh, I'm so proud of all of them. And my, they have rewarded me with such beautiful grandchildren in return for all of my hard work and love."

Sarah listened intently. Unless Abigail was a brilliant criminal mastermind capable of deceiving the most hardened detectives, the woman appeared to be speaking from the heart without any hidden motives. And even more, Sarah thought, Abigail spoke of the son who was a medical researcher without the slightest hesitation. The woman voiced pride in all of her children and clearly delighted in placing them on a pedestal. "I'm sure you have some very beautiful grandchildren, Abigail."

"Oh yes, I do," Abigail confirmed. "My youngest grandchild is seven years old and my oldest is thirty-one. They are all so beautiful and smart. Why, my oldest grandchild took after his papa, my Caleb, and became a medical researcher. Oh, he's so smart."

Sarah threw her eyes at Amanda. "I need to check on Abigail's grandson," she whispered. "Don't let me forget."

Amanda quickly found a pencil and notepad and scribbled down Sarah's words. "Got it."

"Caleb must be so proud," Sarah said in an easy voice. "Do they work together?"

"Oh no," Abigail told Sarah in a pleased tone, "my grandson works for a company that develops those disease shots that help people get better...what do you call them..."

"Vaccines?" Sarah asked.

"Oh yes, that's it," Abigail replied. "Now, my sisters and I have never taken a shot in our adult lives—except for our baby vaccines—we surely believe the human body is capable of taking care of itself without fussing with all that flu vaccine nonsense every year, but he works hard and I am still proud of my grandson."

"I bet you are," Sarah assured Abigail. "Well, it's getting time to go eat dinner. Don't want you to miss Perry Mason! I'll call you in the morning, okay?"

"Okay, dear," Abigail smiled. "My sisters and I will be here...under...what did you call it...oh yes, house arrest. Oh, this is so much fun."

Sarah sighed. She wanted to tell Abigail that murder was no fun at all but knew she would only be wasting her breath. Besides, she had a new investigative lead to explore. "Have a good night."

"Indeed, dear," Abigail promised and hung up.

Sarah slowly put down the phone. "Abigail is either viciously brilliant or just old and innocent," she told Amanda.

"Senile is more like it.," Amanda told Sarah and gestured out the office window. "The diner was still open when we drove past. I better hurry down there and get our dinner before it closes."

"I'll work on opening the box," Sarah said.

"Wait until I get back," Amanda begged. "I want to see what is in there when you open it. Our day is already ruined so we might as well try to add some excitement. Who knows, maybe a wad of cash or a mysterious passport is hidden in that box. Some dark secret from Mitchel's life!"

Sarah glanced at the box. "Unlikely. But okay, June Bug, I'll wait until you come back with our dinner before I open the box."

"Great," Amanda smiled. "Now, love, tell your dear old friend what you would like for dinner," she said, trying to put on the tone of a silly waitress. "Amanda is at your service."

Sarah let out a little laugh. "Just some coffee, a dinner plate and a slice of pie would be nice."

"As you wish, guv'nor," Amanda replied and bundled up to go back out into the storm. "Cheerio," she said and curtsied toward Sarah, "I'll be back in two shakes of a lamb's tail."

"Silly," Sarah laughed. Amanda winked and hurried out of the office, leaving Sarah alone with her thoughts. The first thing Sarah did was call Jacob Bates. "Hello...Mr. Bates...yes, this is Sarah Garland...Spencer."

"What can I do for you?" Jacob Bates asked, standing in a greasy garage staring outside at the storm. He was a man of sixty years and knew from experience that the storm was digging in instead of passing over as the weather report had predicted.

"Mr. Bates, I have a strange request for you," Sarah explained.

"I'm off duty," Jacob informed Sarah. "I'm waiting for the plow to run its last run out front of my garage. I can't get out even if I try."

Sarah locked her eyes on the wooden box. "Good, because my request isn't a tow this time. It involves you going to Mitchel Cochran's truck and checking if you can see any signs that he hauled wood in the bed of his truck."

"How in the world…what for?" Jacob barked at Sarah. He knew all about Sarah's past as a fancy city detective and wasn't too fond of the woman. There were some folks in Snow Falls that liked the woman, but he didn't count himself as one of them. As far as Jacob Bates concerned himself, Sarah Garland…or Spencer, or whatever her last name might be, was a troublemaker who needed to take a long hike back to Los Angeles.

"Please," Sarah asked Jacob. "I…know you don't care for me that much, Mr. Bates, but this isn't a personal request. This is police business. I know you can respect that."

Jacob scratched the back of his neck and then looked down at his gray mechanic's coverall already half unbuttoned; the uniform was grease-stained with time and hard work, work that was respectable. "Police work, huh?" he asked.

"Yes."

"Well, nothing wrong with police work," Jacob told Sarah. "My brother is a cop down in Cheyenne."

"Thank you, Mr. Bates."

"I'll go take a look in the bed of old man Cochran's truck and see what I can find and give you a call," Jacob replied, then tossed the phone down onto a wooden desk that was barely standing. He zipped up his jacket and headed into the tow yard to investigate the truck, leaning into the howling wind with a determined look on his face.

Sarah put down the phone in her hand and studied the brown box. "Where is your key?" she asked, regretting not searching Mitchel Cochran's cabin more thoroughly. However, she reminded herself, the race against the storm had forced her to retreat toward town. "I'll have to make another trip back out to the cabin," she promised herself and then stood up and went to the front room and plopped down behind a computer. "Let's see what we can find out about Abigail's grandson."

Sarah logged into the computer, jumped onto a federal database, and began investigating Abigail's relations until she found Caleb's family and his children. "Jenson O'Healey...age thirty-one. Not married, no children...works for VQY Pharmaceuticals located in...Anchorage?" Sarah pulled her eyes away from the computer. "Anchorage..." she whispered. "VQY Pharmaceuticals...why does that name sound familiar?" Unable to puzzle it out, Sarah focused back on the computer screen and continued to sift through the data about Jenson O'Healey. "Arrest report...let's see. Oh my. Arrested for narcotics distribution at the age of nineteen...a young drug dealer I see. Arrested again at the age of twenty for breaking into a science lab...clear after that, though." She felt suspicion lodged in her gut like a cold stone, yet she could not help but feel lighter to see that the young man's arrest record had cleared up over time. "Okay...graduated from college two years ago...hired on at VQY last year." Sarah rubbed her eyes and took some notes.

"Let's check his work history," she said and began typing on the keyboard. "Here we are...let's see...work history...worked for..." Sarah's eyes went wide. "Worked for Ceiling Properties for four years...age twenty to twenty-four." The connection they had been looking for.

Shocked by her findings, Sarah quickly printed off the information, logged out, and hurried back to Conrad's office. "Pete, please answer," she prayed and snatched up the phone and called her old friend. Pete picked up on the second ring. "Pete, this is Sarah—"

"I knew it was you," Pete groused. "I felt it in my bones."

Sarah grinned. "You old bear," she teased, "you can sense whenever I'm about to cause trouble?"

"I sure can," Pete replied with a cigar stub in his mouth. "I'm standing in my office looking at a bunch of boxes full of my life's work and wondering if I should have really put in my walking papers."

"I think the time arrived, Pete," Sarah answered in an honest voice.

"Me too, kiddo, me too," Pete admitted in a sad voice. "The department has grown too cozy with city hall, it feels corrupt. Same with the politicians. Sure, there's still a few good guys left...but the rotten ones are destroying the honor I swore to uphold for all these years."

"I know, Pete," Sarah said. "Times are changing...people are changing...for the worse. And speaking of people, I need your help—"

"Sarah, our new detective agency isn't even open yet," Pete grumbled. "Give me a break for a few days, okay, before you slap me across the face with demands."

Sarah understood Pete's frustrations and felt guilty. "Okay, Pete, I'm sorry. I wasn't thinking. It was good to hear your voice, though. I can figure this thing out, I'll just—"

"No, no," Pete cut Sarah off as guilt stabbed him in the chest, "just…what is it, huh? I can walk and chew my cigar at the same time."

Sarah quickly sat down and began telling Pete all about the case she was on. She explained about Mitchel Cochran and the O'Healey sisters and her new findings. "Jenson O'Healey worked for Ceiling Properties, the same corrupt property company Mitchel Cochran's daughters owned."

Pete took the cigar out of his mouth, walked behind his old desk, and sat down heavily. "You want me to look deeper into Jenson O'Healey's past, right? Find a few skeletons in his closet?"

"Please."

Pete tossed the cigar down and grabbed up a box of cold Chinese noodles. "Brad McDougal owes me a favor."

"Brad McDougal…from the FBI?"

"Yep," Pete replied, "about the only Fed I can trust. We went through police academy together."

"Okay, Pete," Sarah said and leaned back in Conrad's chair, "let's start digging even deeper and find out what's going on."

"You just focus on the O'Healey sisters and take a shovel to their past and let me worry about my end," Pete ordered Sarah. "If my gut feeling is right, those three women are innocent, like you say. We could be looking at a frame-up scheme here, kiddo."

"That's my fear," Sarah confessed and looked out the office window. Far away in Los Angeles it was warm and sunny, but in Snow Falls it was stormy and growing darker by the second.

Chapter Nine

Sarah was reading a report she had pulled on Jenson O'Healey's dad when Amanda returned from the diner with four bags bulging with to-go plates. "Uh...June Bug, I ordered a dinner plate...not a Thanksgiving meal."

Amanda grinned, set down the bags, stomped snow off her boots, and then removed her hat and gloves. "The diner was preparing to close," she explained. "Melissa gave me all the leftover food and only charged me for two to-go plates and two slices of pie." Amanda tossed her hat and gloves down on the desk. "I like Melissa. She's a sweet girl with a very kind heart."

"Melissa is a sweetheart," Sarah agreed, smelling savory meatloaf and freshly grilled cheeseburgers. "How much food was leftover?"

"I ordered us two meatloaf dinner plates," Amanda explained. "There are ten more to-go plates in those bags...mostly cheeseburger dinners, but beggars can't be choosers."

"No, we can't," Sarah agreed and then tapped the report she was reading. "June Bug, while you were gone, I discovered some very interesting facts."

Amanda began taking off her coat. "Let me defrost, get some food into my tummy, have a hot coffee, and then we'll talk," she promised Sarah. "I also need to call my hubby."

"I understand," Sarah promised and sniffed the air. "The food does smell good."

"My arms were too full to carry drinks. Melissa offered to help me but the poor dear was trying to close the diner as quickly as possible and make it home while she still could," Amanda told Sarah. "We're stuck with coffee and whatever other drinks we can find around this place."

"Coffee will work for me," Sarah said and set down the report she was holding. "Let's go wash up and then we'll eat."

"Deal."

Sarah and Amanda washed their hands in the little kitchenette in the hall and returned to Conrad's office with hungry tummies rumbling at the good smells. Amanda plopped down in her usual chair and grabbed a bag as Sarah positioned herself behind Conrad's desk. "You know," Sarah told Amanda, "I know we're in the middle of a murder case, but in a way, this is kinda like having a girls-only night. We have food, it's snowing so no one is at the station except us, the town is shutting down, people are hurrying home...kinda fun."

Amanda pulled the two meatloaf orders out of the bag in her hand. "I was just thinking about that while I was walking back from the diner," she told Sarah in a warm voice. "Sure, we're stuck watching the station and trying to track down a killer, but besides that, it's kinda cozy. I've always liked being snowed in, just as long as I'm safe and warm and with people I love and trust."

Sarah took a meatloaf container from Amanda and opened it to see the fresh slices of meatloaf and mounds of mashed potatoes covered in gravy and steaming hot buttered green beans and fried okra on the side. "Looks delicious," she said as her mouth began to water. "I'm very particular about meatloaf and only a few places can cook meatloaf the way I like. I would have never believed a small diner in Alaska would cook the world's best meatloaf."

"I know," Amanda giggled. "When I first moved to Snow Falls and visited the diner, I expected greasy food and lousy coffee. I was shocked to find that the bloke in the kitchen was such a gifted chef. The first time I tasted the meatloaf I nearly fainted. And look at this," Amanda gestured to the crispy fried okra. "Cooked to perfection...they never fail to turn out a perfect meal."

"We're definitely blessed to have our diner," Sarah agreed. "Forks?"

Amanda reached into the bag in her lap and pulled out a plastic fork in a bag with little packets of salt and pepper. "Here you go, love."

Sarah took the fork, bowed her head, said a prayer of thanks, and savored her first bite of meatloaf. "Sometimes I miss my favorite diner in Los Angeles," she confessed. "Nostalgia makes me very sad. But then I think about the diner here in Snow Falls and realize that I would miss it if I tried to go back to Los Angeles. It's strange how feelings, old and new, are always at war with each other, tugging at the heart."

Amanda set down the bag she held on the floor, opened

her meatloaf dinner, said a prayer of thanks, and grabbed her own fork. "Sometimes, love, I miss London so much my heart aches with pain. I miss the rain...the fog...the drives my hubby and I used to take in the country." Amanda's face turned wistful as she forked up a piece of meatloaf. "There is a cottage," she continued, "small, cozy and very adorable, that sits out by the Irish Sea. The cottage was owned by an old man and old woman who never left the seaside." Amanda bit into a piece of fried okra and made a delicious sound with her mouth. "One day my hubby and I were driving by and decided to visit the old man and old woman. We were on a short holiday and knew the couple from seeing them in the village from time to time...we weren't very well acquainted, just enough to pay a visit and say hello."

"Sounds lovely."

Amanda sighed. "That day we found the old couple dead," she explained. "They were both lying in bed, holding hands under a homemade quilt...my hubby thought they were asleep but I knew...my heart knew," Amanda told Sarah. "They had died as one heartbeat."

Sarah felt her heart break. "That's very sad."

Amanda shook her head. "They were very old, love, well into their nineties," she said and then continued. "The cottage, much to our shock, was left in my care. Their will was made out all proper."

"June Bug, you never told me this before."

Amanda smiled. "I would have gotten around to it," she promised.

"Do you still have the cottage?" Sarah asked.

"No," Amanda explained as her eyes filled with happiness. "I gave the cottage to a young couple I met walking on the beach. The couple was newly married and just beginning their lives together in the village. I knew that if I kept the cottage it would just fall into ruins—it was too far away for me to visit regularly. So, as a gift of love, I gave the young couple that cottage and made them promise to love each other forever."

Sarah felt a tear fall from her eye. "That's very...touching, June Bug."

"When I was walking back from the diner just now, I thought of that cottage," Amanda told Sarah and smiled at her friend's tear. "It's not the cottage that was special. It was the old man and woman and the love they shared that made the cottage special." Amanda gestured around the office. "This station, by itself, is a drab place. But because it's filled with people I love and care about, well, in a way it's my own little cottage. Just as cozy as if we were in that darling little place by the Irish Sea. I just had to realize that and stop being so pouty thinking our week was ruined."

"You're a very special woman," Sarah told Amanda and raised her fork up into the air. "To family."

"To family," Amanda beamed and dug into her meatloaf. "To family who don't mind how I eat, of course," she giggled.

Sarah laughed. "I wouldn't have it any other way."

Sarah and Amanda both ate their dinners, mostly sitting in silence, listening to the storm outside. When Amanda finished off her meatloaf, she put her take-out container away and let out a polite burp. "My, that was good," she smiled and studied the bags sitting on the floor. "I think I'm going to have to wait for my slice of pie."

"Me, too," Sarah moaned and pushed her container away from her. "I'm stuffed."

Amanda rubbed her tummy. "Better to be stuffed than hungry," she said, pretending to speak in a wise voice.

"Better to be stuffed than hungry," Sarah repeated and then froze. "Oh my," she gasped.

"What?" Amanda asked in an alarmed voice. She darted her eyes around the office. "Did you see someone? Is the killer here? What? What?"

"Mittens' food dish was only half-full when I left the cabin this morning," Sarah explained. "I don't know if she'll have enough food to make it through the night."

"Is that all?" Amanda griped indignantly. "You almost caused me to have a fit because you forgot to fill a feeding dish? Good grief, love, you're going to give me gray hair."

"Mittens has a huge appetite, June Bug," Sarah pointed out, a wrinkle forming in the middle of her forehead the more she thought about it. "She'll go through the dog food I left her in no time. I didn't expect to be gone all day. I hope she doesn't go digging in the garbage…"

"Love," Amanda told Sarah in a stern but caring voice, "Mittens will live until you can feed her."

"I…guess," Sarah said in a worried voice. "She's such a sweet dog and she's used to her feeding times."

Amanda rolled her eyes. "Who owns who?" she asked and then winked at Sarah. "Relax, love, Mittens isn't going to starve to death. We'll drive out to your cabin tomorrow and feed her, okay?"

Sarah thought about the storm howling around them and then nodded. "I'm sure Mr. Rogers will have our road plowed by then."

"Why is it the man who buys the empty cabin on your

road plows for free and the people on my street won't even help me dig out my truck?" Amanda asked with a little pout to her bottom lip.

Sarah began to answer when the phone rang. "Just a second, June Bug," she said and answered the phone. "Hello, this is—"

"It's Pete, kiddo," Pete said, standing on a warm beach so that the waves echoed through his cell phone all the way to Alaska. "Can you talk?"

"Of course."

Pete looked out at the beautiful Pacific bringing in high tide and then gazed up and down an empty and breathtaking beach that only a few lone surfers ever visited. "I'm at our beach."

"You are?" Sarah asked and let out a miserable moan. "Are our rocks still there?"

"Yep," Pete confirmed, feeling a warm breeze touch his face. He glanced up and saw a scrum of seagulls and pelicans gliding in the wind. "Birds are out playing, too."

"Did you bring the seagulls bread?"

"No time to feed the birds today, kiddo. I've got some important news for you," Pete said, growing serious. "I didn't drive way out here to feed some spoiled seabirds."

Sarah leaned forward in Conrad's chair. "What did you find out, Pete?"

"I found out that VQY Pharmaceuticals is under investigation for selling generic pills at suspiciously high prices," Pete explained. "VQY Pharmaceuticals has two locations. One location is in Anchorage and the second location is right here in Los Angeles. And guess what?"

"What?"

"The owner of the company is into real estate and worked with Ceiling Properties," Pete told Sarah. Her silence on the line was testament to the shock she felt at the news. Pete grabbed a cigar stub out of his front pocket and shoved it into his mouth. "In fact, VQY bought some very cheap properties, had them appraised at high prices hardly days later, and sold them off immediately."

"Pete, we're really onto something here," Sarah said in an excited voice. "The pharmaceutical world is major business. Do you think we—"

"Don't get your hopes up, kiddo," Pete cut Sarah off. "VQY is small change compared to the big fish that are out there. VQY makes generic heartburn drugs, beta blockers, antidepressants…nothing major that can contend with the big fish that you see all over the place making billions. VQY only rakes in, at best, a few million a year after costs and production."

Sarah leaned back. "Pete, who owns VQY?"

"Charlie Moorington," Pete told Sarah, strolling down the firm sand and allowing the warm breeze to soothe his mind. "Moorington is a young pup who hasn't reached forty yet. He's a real night-life socialite kinda guy, always in the paparazzi shots with fancy cars and expensive suits."

"I take it he doesn't live in Anchorage."

"No way," Pete said. "Charlie Moorington runs the Los Angeles office. But guess who is in charge of the Anchorage office?"

Sarah sighed heavily and leaned her head into one hand. "Jenson O'Healey?"

"Bingo, kiddo," Pete told Sarah and gnawed on his cigar

again, wishing he could light it but knowing the wind was too strong for a match to stay lit. "That's all I have for now. McDougal is doing some more digging for me. I drove out to our beach because there are too many ears back at the office." Pete looked out at the ocean. "What did you find out on your end?"

"I found out that Jenson O'Healey's dad is a recovering drug addict. The family that seemed so clean and blessed is slowly starting to show signs of trouble."

Pete nodded. "A story on a computer screen can make anyone look clean, kiddo. But when you start to dig under the surface, you find some ugly dirt. It's that way for everybody. No one is clean except the good Lord. The rest of us are all just...messy. Some of us wise up, though, and get clean while the rest just stay dirty."

Sarah looked at Amanda. Amanda, in her eyes, had a clean heart, one that was a blessing to witness. But she had a feeling Pete was in no mood for happy stories just at the moment. "Pete, Jenson O'Healey's dad was fired from his job three years ago for drug use. This didn't show on the first database I used to look at him. I had to use...uh...a separate database—"

"You mean you hacked into a secure database the Feds don't like people seeing?"

"You're the one who taught me how to hack into places," Sarah said in a proud voice.

"I should be shot."

Sarah grinned. "We both should have been shot for trying to be good cops."

"Tell me something I don't know," Pete told Sarah. "But before we shoot ourselves maybe you better tell me what you found out."

"I'm sure McDougal is going to discover this, but you can get a jump on him," Sarah told Pete.

Pete chewed on his cigar. "I'm ready, kiddo. Hit me."

"I found out that Jenson O'Healey's dad is working at VQY," Sarah told Pete.

"Now that is interesting," Pete said and whistled.

"It sure is," Sarah agreed. She glanced at the office window. "Pete, right now we're pinned down by another snowstorm. There's not much I can do until tomorrow. I have the O'Healey sisters under house arrest—"

"Did you check the dead man's place?" Pete asked in a quick voice.

"Pete, you know better than to ask me that. You're the man who trained me," Sarah replied.

"What did you find?"

"A wooden box. I still haven't opened it," Sarah explained.

"Locked?"

"Yes," Sarah confirmed. "But if you hang on a minute, I'll break the box open and tell you what's inside."

"Call me back when you find out what's in the box, kiddo," Pete told Sarah. "I want to walk down to the water and try to get my cigar lit and rest my mind a bit. Filling out all my retirement paperwork has worn me down. I'm so close now."

"Okay, Pete," Sarah promised, "I'll call you right back."

"No rush," Pete said with a sigh that belied his age and fatigue. "This old man isn't going anywhere."

Sarah stiffened. "Pete, are you okay?" she asked in a concerned voice. There was a pause and the seagull cries and waves in the background soothed her even though her heart ached for her friend.

Finally, he replied. "Just tired, kiddo, and...not ready to let go. It's going to take time," Pete told Sarah and ended the call.

Sarah slowly hung up the phone. "Looks like we're not the only ones trapped in a storm," she told Amanda and felt her worry for Pete begin to gnaw a small but significant hole in her stomach.

Chapter Ten

Sarah studied the lock on the wooden box like a cat burglar studying a jewelry vault. "The lock is basic," she told Amanda. "But," she added, "this box isn't cheap. The quality is solid." She shifted it around and felt the heavy woodwork, the precise joining at each corner.

Amanda sipped her cup of coffee. "Why don't we just take a hammer and smash the box open?" she asked, standing next to Sarah.

Sarah was tempted to grab Amanda's suggestion and run with it. But she reminded herself the box was evidence that would most likely need to be used in a court of law—assuming that she found something critical inside the box. It should not be smashed up unless it was the absolute last option. "June Bug, I need to preserve this as evidence. Let me see if I can fiddle with the lock before we take drastic measures."

Amanda studied a couple metal picks and the screwdriver and hammer Sarah had managed to locate in a supply closet.

"I give you two minutes before you get frustrated and smash the box open."

Sarah raised her eyes up to Amanda and set her jaw stubbornly with a grin. "You're on. If I win, you buy me a new outfit."

Amanda grinned. "If I win, you buy me two."

"Deal," Sarah grinned as they shook on it. She snatched up the screwdriver and picks and went to work. Amanda plopped down in her chair, sipped her coffee, and watched Sarah as her mind began to wonder what two dresses she wanted from O'Mally's. Just when she had settled on the first dress, a soft red brocade velvet that would be perfect for the holidays, the clasp of the wooden box made a metallic *click*, and then the wooden lid eased open an inch. "Oh," she pouted.

Sarah tossed the screwdriver down on the desk, turned around, and brushed off her hands. "First thing a good cop learns to do is pick a simple lock. I can't tell you how many hours I stood in front of my bathroom door back in Los Angeles picking the lock."

"Why the bathroom door?" Amanda asked.

Sarah let out an embarrassed giggle. "I figured that if I had to use the bathroom bad enough I would pick the lock one way or another. No better way to learn." She grinned. "I kept the floor dry, I'll say that much."

"Smart girl," Amanda complimented Sarah and then narrowed her eyes, "but unfortunately I'm going to have to cry foul. You tricked me, love."

"I did not," Sarah said in a pretend shocked voice. "I just didn't tell you that I had experience picking locks."

Amanda pointed her finger at Sarah like a school teacher

about to discipline a wayward child. "You're a very tricky woman, Los Angeles. I know your kind. You're like a pool shark. You like to draw in innocent bystanders such as myself and then steal our money."

Sarah folded her arms. "June Bug, when it comes to shopping, you're about as innocent as a spider in a room full of flies. Why, when there is a sale taking place...watch out, because you'll tear someone's arm off if they try to reach for a blouse you're going for."

Amanda displayed a proud smile. "Twenty percent off is twenty percent off," she replied. "I just so happened to save myself over forty dollars during the last sale O'Mally's offered."

"You also bumped poor Mrs. Lakes out of the way with your elbow trying to get a lovely pink blouse."

"Oh yeah...kinda forgot about that," Amanda blushed. "I was caught up in the moment and fighting my way through the mad crowds."

"June Bug, Mrs. Lakes was the only person in the clothing section," Sarah laughed.

"Oh yeah...I guess she was," Amanda blushed again.

"Just never forget the wallop she gave you with her cane," Sarah laughed again.

Amanda closed her eyes and saw the angry old woman who had smacked her backside with a hard wooden cane. "Yeah...ouch," she grimaced.

Sarah rolled her eyes and turned her attention to the wooden box. "Okay, June Bug, let's see what's in the box."

Amanda stood up and joined Sarah. "I'm ready."

Sarah opened the lid. She was disappointed not to find an

old fashioned treasure of gold or jewels, but at least the box was not empty. "Well, will you look at this," she said, lifting out a white envelope. She opened it and shook out a single key.

"A key?" Amanda asked. "Now why would Mitchel Cochran keep a key locked in a sturdy box under his bed?"

"I'm not sure," Sarah responded, studying the key in her hand with careful eyes. "By the way, Jacob Bates from the garage called me before you returned from the diner. He said he found evidence that Mr. Cochran was hauling wood in his truck."

"He did?" Amanda asked. "What kind of evidence? Why didn't you tell me?"

"I was going to tell you. I got distracted," Sarah apologized. She handed Amanda the key. "I know Mr. Cochran was far too old to haul and stack all the wood we saw at his cabin by himself. Of course, he was a hardy old-timer and I could be wrong. I have learned to never jump to conclusions." Sarah folded her arms. "A lot of new data is emerging and I'm trying to digest it very carefully. But it's important that the man's own truck seemed to be scratched up and dented, just like he was carrying lots of wood back and forth. Jacob said he had no doubt about that. There were even splinters of leftover wood and such in the truck bed, under the snow. However, as far as we know, that could simply mean that he used his truck to haul some of the wood from his side yard up to the front porch. Who knows?"

Amanda studied the key in her hand. "Love, this key looks so familiar," she puzzled.

"I have a key that looks like that as well."

Amanda looked up at Sarah, comprehension dawning in her eyes. "The storage units out on Snow Deer Road."

Sarah nodded. "Exactly," she said, grabbing her coffee to take a big sip. "June Bug, I've been careful not to jump to conclusions here...but the more evidence we collect the more it appears that Mr. Cochran wasn't walking this mysterious road alone. There's some kind of shadow person, or persons, who must have been working with him."

Amanda tossed the key back into the envelope in the wooden box and sat back in her chair. "Do you believe this shadow killed Mitchel?" she asked.

Sarah shrugged her shoulders. "Mr. Cochran was alive when I left the coffee shop," she replied. "You heard the front door to the coffee shop open. When you went to refill Mr. Cochran's coffee you saw the O'Healey sisters standing over his body."

"Mitchel's head was down on the table," Amanda confirmed. "I asked one of the sisters if Mitchel was alright but all they did was smile in that creepy way they have. That's when I checked his pulse...I knew the old man was dead and hurried to call you."

Sarah bit down on her lip. "Which certainly points to the O'Healeys being the killers," she said in a frustrated voice. "I have no evidence other than a gut feeling that someone was standing in the shadows with Mr. Cochran. I have plenty of evidence that could easily plaster the guilty label on the O'Healey sisters...but it doesn't feel right."

"The O'Healey sisters did confess to killing Mitchel," Amanda pointed out.

"I know...I know," Sarah responded, forcing her mind to remain focused instead of becoming clouded with irritation.

"June Bug, we need to break this case down and focus on one section at a time," she explained. "For the moment I'm going to assume that someone hiding in the shadows killed Mr. Cochran and is trying to pin the murder on the O'Healey sisters." Sarah sipped at her coffee. "We do have evidence that connects Abigail Healey's son and grandson to Mr. Cochran's daughters. I want to focus on that."

"You're the boss," Amanda agreed.

"And so are you," Sarah pointed out. "You're a very clever woman, June Bug. Don't take a back seat on me."

Amanda smiled. "I wouldn't dream of it," she promised and blushed at Sarah's compliment. "Here's a question…were the Cochran daughters in town? Or Abigail's son or grandson?"

"We don't have any evidence of that so far…" Sarah peered out the office window. "The storm is too strong to drive out to the storage units tonight. That might be where we'll find out about the Cochran daughters at least…but we'll have to wait until tomorrow."

"So what do we do in the meantime?" Amanda asked and then quickly read Sarah's eyes. "Oh, you want to call VQY Pharmaceuticals, don't you?"

"The thought has crossed my mind," Sarah admitted. "I need to see if Jenson O'Healey is in Anchorage. I also want to find out more about Mr. Cochran's daughters. Records show that they are both living in Los Angeles. But I didn't even get a work history on either of them."

"Are you thinking Mitchel's daughters are working for VQY Pharmaceuticals in Los Angeles?"

"I told you, you're a brilliant woman," Sarah beamed. "Why don't we go and find out and then we call Anchorage?"

"Oh, this is getting fun," Amanda confessed. "Uh...no offense to poor Mitchel. Rest in peace."

"I'm sure Mr. Cochran would want us to do everything within our power to solve his murder," Sarah assured Amanda and they walked back to the desk where she had been looking up information earlier. "I'm going to have to do some more...hacking," she confessed.

Amanda's eyes popped. "Can I watch and learn?"

"I thought you would never ask. Pull up a chair," Sarah told Amanda in a happy voice. Amanda quickly slid a chair over to the desk and sat down. Sarah drew in a steady breath, stretched her hands, and said: "Here we go."

"Here we go," Amanda said, feeling like she was on a roller coaster ride. She watched Sarah place her fingertips down on the black keyboard and start working. There were at least three different places she needed to check, and ways to hack into each of them by guessing passwords or accessing the data directly, and Sarah's hands flew as she skillfully navigated a dizzying blur of data. Twenty minutes later, Sarah stopped typing and tapped the computer screen. "VQY Pharmaceuticals," she whispered.

Sarah nodded in awe and calculated a rough timeline based on the dates they saw on the screen. "Alicia and Mandy Cochran began working at VQY shortly after they were released from prison."

"But how? VQY was connected to their real estate scheme somehow?" Amanda asked.

"My guess is Charlie Moorington has some big players in his corner that made a judge turn a blind eye. I'm also guessing he wanted to keep his enemies close."

"Which means the Cochran sisters must be in Los Angeles, right?" Amanda asked.

"Unless they want to break their probation," Sarah explained, "they better be."

Amanda stared at the computer screen and then looked at Sarah. "There's more to this than you're telling me," she said, reading Sarah's eyes.

"I don't want to jump to conclusions, but my guess is the O'Healey and Cochran families are connected in more ways than Abigail, Betty and Martha understand. My guess is," Sarah ventured, "that Alicia and Mandy Cochran are two very clever women who understand how to get what they want from people, including their sworn enemies."

"Are you talking about blackmail?" Amanda asked.

"Yes," Sarah said. "The Cochran sisters are about the same age as Caleb O'Healey. Caleb O'Healey lived in Los Angeles for most of his adult life." Sarah rubbed her nose. "Abigail said she already contacted her children to let them know Mitchel Cochran was dead. I wanted to press Abigail on that issue but decided to wait until later."

Amanda stared at the computer screen. "Can you find the man's phone number?" she asked.

"I've already located a company cell phone number for both Caleb and Jenson O'Healey," Sarah told Amanda, typing quickly.

"Just now?"

Sarah nodded. "I work fast."

"Wow," Amanda gasped, "you do work fast."

"It's not difficult once you get into a secure database," Sarah explained. "The hard part is breaking in through a back door without being heard. Pete taught me a few tricks that still work, but it's getting tough. Back in the old days it was easier. Technology is rapidly changing, and soon I won't be able to outsmart a computer."

"I hate computers," Amanda admitted. "I think they are awful little creatures that serve no other purpose than to allow me to shop for dresses online. I despise technology in general. Oh, not the lights and central heat and air. I despise the bad stuff...all these new phones, gadgets, tablets, televisions. When I was a little girl, I called someone from home and didn't carry a phone out with me. I wrote letters and used stamps. Sure, technology offers convenience, but it destroys the old ways. When I was a little girl we played outside and gathered around the fireplace at night to talk and have a cup of tea as a family."

"I know what you mean," Sarah sighed. "Every kid I see these days seems to spend their time with their face shoved into a phone, computer screen, tablet or some other piece of technology that is draining the life out of their youth. While we were in Los Angeles I...secretly visited my old house...walked around my old neighborhood." Sarah printed a few pages and then exited the secure database and looked at Amanda. "I didn't see kids outside playing. What I did see was a bunch of teenagers walking around with their faces glued to their phones."

"It's getting to be that way here in Snow Falls, too," Amanda said in a disappointed voice. "Last week when I visited O'Mally's, I saw a group of kids sitting in the snack area." Amanda shook her head. "Los Angeles, the kids I saw were all on their phones doing something...not one kid was talking. It was like watching a bunch of robots."

"The world is changing for the worse," Sarah nodded. "The O'Healey sisters grew up blessed. They grew in a time where they understood what it felt like to climb a tree or walk barefoot in a mountain stream or pick wild blackberries. I'm very envious of them."

"You know what?" Amanda confessed, "so am I."

Sarah began to speak when she heard the front door to the station open. To her shock, she saw Dr. Milton stumble in. Dr. Milton tried to raise his right hand up into the air and say something, but before a word could leave his mouth he collapsed down onto the floor, his head slumping at a strange angle.

"Dr. Milton!" Sarah yelled. She jumped to her feet, ran to Dr. Milton, dropped down onto her knees and began feeling for a pulse. "I got a pulse...he's alive."

Amanda rushed to close the front door. As she did, her eyes spotted someone standing across the street under a street lamp. "Los Angeles!" she hollered over her shoulder, "there's someone across the street staring at the door...come and look!"

Sarah bolted to her feet, ran to the front door, and stared out into the storm. She spotted a strange figure dressed in a heavy black ski coat running away. Sarah quickly drew out her gun. "Stay here," she ordered Amanda, grabbing a jacket off the coat rack next to the front door and slinging it on.

Before Amanda could say a word, Sarah burst out into the storm, the jacket not even zipped up and the wind and snow whipping against her winter dress. She raced across the street through deep drifts of snow up to her knees.

Amanda glanced over her shoulder at Dr. Milton. "Oh my," she said in a scared voice, "tonight is going a very different way than I thought...we're in trouble."

Outside in the snow, Sarah focused her attention on the unknown person who was already far ahead of her. Whoever she was chasing, she thought, the person sure could run. "I'm not going to catch up," she panted, her breaths heaving in white clouds of fog, and slid to a stop as she watched the stranger slip around a street corner and vanish. Miserably, she turned and fought her way back through the heavy snow to the police station, wondering how they were going to catch a killer.

Chapter Eleven

Dr. Milton rubbed the back of his head, shivering. "I probably have a mild concussion," he groaned painfully.

Sarah handed Dr. Milton a warm, wet washcloth. "What happened, Dr. Milton?" she asked, staring down at a weakened man dripping with snow. The poor man was very pale and obviously shaken up.

Sarah watched Dr. Milton apply the wet washcloth to the back of his head and check for blood. "Are you okay?" she asked in a worried voice.

"Weak and somewhat dizzy," Dr. Milton explained. He removed the washcloth and checked it. "A little blood, not much. The blood coming from the gash on the back of my head is slowly stopping. I guess I'm lucky I was lying in the snow for a while…" He slowly made his way to his feet and Sarah and Amanda together helped him stagger to an easy chair in Conrad's office where they could talk.

"Do you know who attacked you?" Sarah asked when the man was settled on the chair, wrapped in a few old blankets they found in a back storeroom. His shivering slowly calmed as the warmth seeped back into his body.

Dr. Milton shook his head. "Mrs. Spencer, the phones at the hospital went out. It's possible a tree fell on the phone lines. It wouldn't be the first time," Dr. Milton began to speak. "I needed to speak with you. The matter was very urgent. I knew the last plow of the day already went through, but I decided to brave the roads anyway. When I reached my truck, I...someone hit me from behind." Dr. Milton placed the wet washcloth back on his wound. "I woke up in the back of my truck. When I leaned up, I noticed that my truck was close to town...right in town, to be more accurate. I saw the blood in the snow under my head...I somehow managed to jump out into the snow...like a madman, I must admit. I was terrified, half numb with cold and fear, but I had to get away in case whoever hit me was waiting to do something worse."

"And you ran to the station?" Sarah asked.

Dr. Milton nodded. "Yes."

Sarah rubbed her chin. "Someone was waiting at the hospital for you, Dr. Milton. Someone who doesn't want you speaking the truth."

Dr. Milton winced in pain. "Mrs. Spencer, I was wrong," he said.

"Wrong?" Sarah asked.

"Wrong?" Amanda echoed Sarah.

Dr. Milton removed the washcloth and accepted the hot coffee Amanda offered him. "The poison," he said and took a careful sip of the coffee. "The poison doesn't cause an immediate heart attack by itself. Yes, it is true Mitchel Cochran's heart enzymes were saturated with the poison, but after careful study I realized the poison was a type that cannot be activated unless it is triggered."

"Triggered?" Amanda asked. "Oh dear."

"Yes. The trigger, in this case, would have to be something inhaled—that's the only way the trigger could reach the man's bloodstream quickly and in sufficient quantity." The doctor wrapped his fingers around the hot coffee gratefully.

Sarah walked behind Conrad's desk and sat down. "A trigger he inhaled. A trigger such as...let's say...perfume," she said in a thoughtful voice. "Perfume might be worn by an old lady." She glanced at Amanda meaningfully.

"Perfume, cologne, smelling salts, whatever the trigger may be. You see," Dr. Milton explained, "the poison is a stick of dynamite missing a fuse."

Sarah grew silent for a minute. "Dr. Milton, if Mr. Cochran had ingested the poison but had never been exposed to the trigger, would he still be alive?"

"Most likely," Dr. Milton agreed. "While it's true the poor man did die of a sudden, massive heart attack caused by the trigger chemical, all he would have suffered from the poison alone would have been some chest pains, at most."

"How long does the poison stay in a person's system?"

"The poison is very potent and saturates the heart tissue," Dr. Milton explained. He took another sip of coffee and shivered again. "I would say, in my honest medical opinion, the poison could be dangerous, able to be triggered, for up to three to five days, maybe a day or two longer depending on if he was being given regular doses of it, say. But from what I saw on the blood test, it appeared that Mitchel ingested the poison very recently, within the last twenty-four hours, to be exact."

"Dr. Milton, have you spoken to anyone about these

findings today?" Sarah asked. "Coworkers, professional contacts, anyone besides Amanda and me?"

Dr. Milton put down his coffee to pull the blankets tighter around his shoulders. "Mitchel's daughters contacted me," he explained and quickly closed his eyes and waited for a wave of trembling to pass. "I spoke to them for about half an hour and explained to them that Mitchel was killed by a very deadly poison." Dr. Milton finally opened his eyes. "I assured his daughters that I was going to track down what kind of poison it was and that this information would assist the authorities in finding the killer."

Sarah looked at Amanda. Amanda nodded. "I think it's time we call a few company cell phones," she said.

"You bet it is," Sarah agreed. She snatched up a piece of paper off her desk and then picked up the telephone. "I'll contact Caleb O'Healey first."

"Always go to the parent," Amanda agreed.

Dr. Milton closed his eyes again, confused. "I want answers," he demanded in a weak voice. "Someone tried to kill me."

"Be patient," Sarah urged Dr. Milton and dialed Caleb O'Healey's company mobile number. Caleb picked up on the first ring.

"Jenson?"

"No, this isn't Jenson, Mr. O'Healey. This is Detective Sarah Garland...Spencer," Sarah spoke in a firm and clear voice.

Caleb Jenson met her words with panicked, paralyzed silence. "What...can I do for you, Detective?" he finally asked, clearing his throat. "This is a private business number. I am expecting...an urgent business call." Caleb kicked himself for answering an unknown number calling from Alaska. But who else would be calling him from there? Who else had his cell phone number? "We need to make this quick. I'm a very busy man. I have a flight to catch…" He hurriedly thought about escaping from Anchorage back to Los Angeles.

"Mr. O'Healey, I'm calling from the Snow Falls Police Department."

"I see," Caleb replied and paused awkwardly before continuing. "Oh, I see," he said again, agitation and worry seeming to color his words. "Are you calling in regards to my mother? Is she alright? Please tell me nothing has happened to her."

Sarah felt sadness strike her heart. As much as Abigail loved her children, she thought, it was clear that at least one of her children did not return that love with good intentions. "Abigail O'Healey is…in trouble," Sarah told Caleb, interested now to hear if he would even be disturbed to hear such news. "I'm calling you, Mr. O'Healey, because I saw your son in town. I tried to speak with him about this matter, but he… fled on foot before we could chat."

Amanda grinned. Sarah was being delightfully clever. "Get 'em, girl," she whispered.

Caleb's polished, tough exterior began to show cracks. "I— uh, my son…I'm sorry, you said you saw my son?" All his intelligence and intimidation faded and on the inside, Caleb O'Healey felt like a nervous wreck; a man on the verge of a mental breakdown. The last thing he needed was for his son to mess up. "I'm sorry my son was so rude," he said brusquely. "He is in town visiting his grandmother and his great-aunts. Perhaps he was simply…eager to get back to see them."

"I see," Sarah replied. "I suppose he takes his work with

him when he travels? After all, you were expecting an important business call from him, right? I mean, Jenson O'Healey works at VQY, right?"

Caleb choked on his words. "Detective—"

"Spencer."

"Detective Spencer, my son is a very important man at work...he makes it a point to stay in touch with me concerning important business matters. It isn't a crime for a man to take his work with him," Caleb said, his mouth running a mile a minute as he sought for a way out.

Sarah listened to the man talk and knew exactly what this fancy businessman was contemplating: a cowardly act. He was going to run. "No, it's not a crime to be an alcoholic...oh dear, wrong word..." Sarah chuckled. "I'm so sorry. What I meant to say is that it's not a crime to be a workaholic. Of course he can take work on the road."

Caleb sputtered, grasping for a shred of his former power. "Detective Spencer, I'll inform my son that he needs to contact you. Now, I'm afraid I must go...flight to catch...I'm a very busy man..."

Sarah looked at Amanda. It was time to lower the boom. "Are you?" she asked. "I assumed you would be celebrating."

"Celebrating?" Caleb asked.

"Your mother did call you, didn't she?" Sarah asked.

"My mother hasn't contacted me," Caleb lied.

"That's strange," Sarah replied and leisurely took a sip of her coffee. "Abigail told me she contacted all of her children and told them that the family feud between the Greenlights and the Cochrans had finally come to an end...with the death of Mitchel Cochran, of course."

Caleb sounded out of breath, running while he spoke into

the mobile phone. "Detective Spencer, my mother has not contacted me—"

"Mr. O'Healey, Mitchel Cochran was poisoned to death and your mother and her two sisters are being blamed," Sarah snapped, throwing her politeness out into the snow. "I know they didn't kill Mitchel Cochran. I do know, however, who did. So if you want to avoid prison, you better cut the cowardice and talk to me. And if you're thinking about fleeing to Los Angeles, don't bother, because I have cops at the Anchorage airport waiting for you." It was a bluff, but she needed to press him.

Caleb froze with his hand on the door of his BMW. "I..." he began to speak but stopped. What was a man in his position supposed to say? "I...wish to consult my lawyer," he finally spoke.

"No deal," Sarah snapped in a harsh voice. She was tired of the O'Healey family remaining silent on her. "Talk to me or go to prison. I know the district attorney here and I can make it so you wish you and your family never came to Snow Falls. I'm the only person who can help you."

Caleb dropped the briefcase in his hand and wobbled down onto the floor of the parking garage. "It was all a mistake," he whispered. "I warned Alicia and Mandy it wouldn't work..."

"What wouldn't work?" Sarah demanded.

"Everything!" Caleb nearly began crying, then took a shuddering breath and tried again. "Years ago, Alicia Cochran and I were in love. We were going to get married but...we couldn't."

"Because of the feud?" Sarah asked.

"Mitchel Cochran would have killed me with his bare

hands...my own parents would have killed me," Caleb whimpered. "I was a young man of twenty...Alicia was so young and beautiful...we loved each other. It was so long ago…we're both in our fifties now..." Caleb shuddered with a sigh.

"Keep talking to me, Mr. O'Healey."

Caleb wiped his left hand over his sweaty, tearful face. "It was for the best anyway. I later found out Alicia never loved me...all she wanted was the gold."

"What gold?" Sarah asked.

"The gold that Stephen Greenlight...killed Billy Cochran over," Caleb confessed in a condemned voice. "Billy Cochran stole gold from the Greenlights. He stole Stephen Greenlight's claim. And Alicia was going to marry me just for revenge. I was stupid enough to believe in her promises. There, are you happy? Isn't that enough?"

Sarah put down her coffee. "Mr. Caleb, you have to keep going. Keep talking to me."

Caleb's body began to shake so bad he felt like he was going to fall out of his skin. "You wouldn't understand," he insisted. He climbed into the plush leather seat of his BMW just so he could have someplace to hide. "You don't understand."

"Oh, I think I might," Sarah assured Caleb. "I think this goes back to a time before you were born. After Miren Cochran left Stephen Greenlight after her daddy stole the gold, Stephen Greenlight set it in his mind to kill Billy Cochran and take back his wife and the gold. Is that about right?"

"How...did you know?" Caleb whispered in a shocked voice.

"I'm a detective," Sarah explained. "It's my job to figure these things out." And maybe knock some sense into two crazy families while I'm at it, she told herself.

Caleb palmed sweat off his forehead again. "Alicia...all she wanted was the gold. Alicia and Mandy found me later, after I had married and had a son. They began stalking my wife until..." he gulped.

"Until what?"

"Until my wife finally left me," Caleb cried. "I never told my mother that. How could I? My mother thinks I'm a prince. I couldn't tell her my wife was scared away by the Cochran girls, after all these years."

"We'll focus on that later," Sarah promised. "What else did the Cochran sisters do?"

Caleb licked his dry lips. "Alicia and Mandy slowly began to destroy my life. They got me fired from my job. Made me lose my house. I...began drinking," Caleb confessed. "I became a horrible parent to my son...I wasn't even aware he was using illegal drugs...drugs supplied by Alicia and Mandy, I later found out..."

Sarah listened to Caleb speak. As she did, a sudden realization struck her. "Mr. O'Healey, is Mr. Moorington, the man who owns VQY, related to Alicia and Mandy Cochran?"

Caleb's violent shaking increased as he took in how much trouble he was truly in. "How did you know? Yes. Charlie Moorington belongs to Miren Cochran's bloodline. Miren Cochran remarried after she divorced Stephen Greenlight." Caleb grabbed his knees with his left hand and tried to stop them from shaking. "Charlie Moorington is a dangerous man...power-hungry...money-hungry...but he has a very bad gambling problem. VQY would be a decent company and a real competitor if he would allow me to make proper investments instead of gambling away all of our profits." Caleb shook his head. "Listen to me talking like I honestly care for this company. I'm working for VQY only because I'm being threatened."

"By who?"

"My own son," Caleb confessed in a tortured voice, a sob breaking through his words. "Jenson has taken sides with Alicia and Mandy and Charlie Moorington. They all want the gold…the gold worth hundreds of millions…gold that Stephen Greenlight buried somewhere in the Alaskan wilderness. Or so Mitchel Cochran claimed, but Alicia and Mandy said he was lying."

Sarah felt a surge of questions enter her mind but stayed focused on the current path Caleb was taking her down. "Did they kill Mitchel Cochran over it?"

Caleb squeezed his eyes closed. "No…I did," he whimpered. "I created the poison…and the trigger. I didn't have a choice. My life was being threatened."

"Mr. O'Healey, you didn't administer the poison to Mr. Cochran, did you?"

"No," Caleb whimpered again. "My son…Jenson…that was his job."

"Explain."

Caleb tried to make his hands stop shaking. "Alicia and Mandy convinced Mitchel to hire somebody to help him…a handy man of sorts. Mitchel was an old man and he couldn't perform chores like he used to. The daughters made it sound like they were just trying to help him in his old age. At first he rebelled, and then agreed."

"Jenson O'Healey became Mr. Cochran's new helper, is that right?" Sarah asked.

"Yes," Caleb confessed. "My son...his job was to administer the poison after I set up...my mother and my aunts."

"You mean after you framed three innocent women for murder?"

Caleb let out a miserable cry. "I tried to fight Alicia and Mandy on that...I was the reason they went to prison for real estate fraud. I stole papers from my son—"

"Your son was working with Alicia and Mandy."

"Yes," Caleb cried. "I stole papers and turned them over to the authorities. I thought I was finished with them. But then Charlie Moorington showed up at my door. He threatened to kill my son...and even promised to track down my ex-wife and kill her if I didn't do as he ordered. I didn't have a choice. I— they all believe my mother knows where the gold is. Charlie Moorington himself refused to let me go until I—"

Sarah heard Caleb's voice cut out as the phone line went silent. She looked up at Amanda. "The phone call just went dead," she said and went for her gun. "I didn't hear any trees falling, which means one thing."

"Oh my...here we go," Amanda said in a dreadful voice as the night finally took full control of the storm.

Chapter Twelve

Sarah eased through the back door of the station with her gun at the ready. Icy winds and heavy snow spotted her and began a vicious assault. "Stay close," Sarah called back to Amanda.

Amanda quickly checked the flashlight she held and then bravely stepped outside. Sure, she thought, feeling the winds and snow rush at her face in fierce anger, there was a killer loose in the storm—again—but she was through being afraid. If being the best friend of Sarah Garland...Spencer...had taught her anything, it was that you had to face life with your fists ready. Even though deep inside of her heart Amanda was very afraid, she refused to let out a single whimper. "I'm right behind you," she promised.

Sarah turned right and began trudging through knee-high snow. "The phone line is this way," she yelled, peering into the darkness. If the killer was lurking in the dark, she couldn't spot him. Amanda held onto the flashlight with one hand and grabbed Sarah's shoulder with the other, her head ducked down against the deadly winds. Sarah carefully led the way to the phone line and stopped. "Shine the light here," she hollered.

"Okay," Amanda hollered back and threw the flashlight beam at a gray metal box affixed to the side of the brick station. "Look!"

"I see it!" Sarah yelled over the winds. She reached out her gloved right hand and grabbed a black phone wire dangling from the gray box. "The phone line has been cut."

Amanda turned her head away from Sarah and explored the night. "The storm is getting worse by the second. We better get back inside. I don't think I've seen it this horrible in years."

"I know," Sarah yelled. "The storm is turning into a hurricane blizzard. Come on." Sarah grabbed Amanda's arm and together they fought their way back inside the station. "Goodness," she said, closing the door and putting her gun away, "I've never seen it like this before."

"Me neither," Amanda said in a worried voice and began stomping snow off her boots. "The storm eased off us for a little bit earlier this afternoon but then returned with vengeance."

"We call a storm like this a White Killer," Dr. Milton spoke.

Sarah jerked her head up and spotted Dr. Milton standing in the short hallway leading to the back door. "Dr. Milton, you should be resting."

Dr. Milton ignored Sarah. "I've lived through one White Killer before," he frowned. "When the storm ended, the town of Ice Creek Falls was totally destroyed." Dr. Milton paused and listened to the winds and snow pound the station. "The temperature drops so fast a man's body can freeze to ice within minutes. The winds are so powerful that they sheer trees right off the hillside and cut a man in half like a hungry bear tearing apart a lost hunter. The snow builds and builds...and blinds you. A person who has walked to his mailbox a thousand times can become lost within seconds by the blinding snow...turned around...confused...and then...dead."

Sarah listened to the storm. "Well...at least half the town is sick, which means people will be indoors," she said in a hopeless voice.

"At least some people in Snow Falls will have enough sense to stay indoors," Dr. Milton agreed. "Ice Creek Falls was located close to a ski resort. People thought the storm was fun...they were wrong."

Amanda felt a cold chill run down her spine. "Dr. Milton, maybe you should go and lay back down in one of those empty cells?" she asked. "I'm afraid it's not much, but it's better than sitting upright in a chair all night."

"As long as we stay inside, we'll be safe," Dr. Milton said. "You ladies were blessed to make it back inside as it is." And with those words, he walked away.

"Isn't this lovely," Amanda complained and marched back to Conrad's office, dropped down in her chair, grabbed a bag from the diner, dug out a cheeseburger and took a bite. "We're trapped...again."

Sarah took off her gloves and tossed them down onto the desk. "The station has a backup generator that should kick on if the power goes out. So far, we're okay."

"So far, we're trapped with a killer on the loose...again," Amanda continued to fuss.

Sarah pulled out the top desk drawer, retrieved her purse, and tried her cell phone. "Nothing," she said.

"We won't have service in this storm, love."

"A girl can hope," Sarah sighed and tossed her phone down. "Well, June Bug, we may be trapped, but at least we made progress." Sarah studied the food bags. "May I have a cheeseburger? Believe it or not, I'm still hungry."

Amanda dug Sarah out a cheeseburger box and placed it on the desk. "You're worried about Caleb O'Healey, aren't you?" she asked. "When you're worried, you get hungry and eat, just like me."

"I'm sure he's vanished into the wind by now," Sarah confessed. "I had the man right where I wanted him, June Bug. He was giving me all the answers I needed...and then..." Sarah hit the desk with her fist. "I'm going to catch Jenson O'Healey if it's the last thing I do."

"Not in this storm, love," Amanda responded in a cautious voice. "You heard Dr. Milton."

"I heard every word Dr. Milton spoke, June Bug," Sarah sighed and grabbed her cheeseburger plate and opened it. "If we're trapped inside, that means Jenson O'Healey has to be trapped inside somewhere, too. This storm has put us at a stalemate for tonight." Sarah picked up a handful of french fries. "I'm sure he went to hunker down someplace safe after he cut the phone line."

"Let's hope," Amanda told Sarah. She took a bite of her cheeseburger and listened to the storm. As she did, the lights began to flicker and then went out. "Oh my."

Sarah, out of instinct, went for her gun. Before she unholstered it, the generator kicked on and the lights returned. "Oh, thank God," Sarah said in a relieved voice, "the generator is working."

"Good thing Andrew had the generator checked and

rewired last month," Amanda said. "The entire connector...cord...thingy...was severed."

"Yeah, good thing," Sarah sighed as her thoughts turned to Mittens. "I hope my baby is okay. She hates the dark."

"So do I," Amanda pointed out.

Sarah leaned back in her chair and munched on a couple fries. "June Bug, I don't mind snowstorms," she confessed. "As a matter of fact, I enjoy them. Being trapped in a snowstorm forces the world to stand back for a while...and you become part of an entirely new world...a world of white wonder."

"Is that the writer talking?" Amanda asked.

"I suppose it is," Sarah replied and polished off her fries. "Snow is very enchanting to me," she explained. "Snow transforms an ordinary town like Snow Falls into a mysterious delight. Everything looks new and different. Inside the snow you can...be free from the world." Sarah looked at Amanda. "After my first husband divorced me, that's all I wanted...to be free from the world."

Amanda saw hurt in Sarah's eyes. "I know, love."

Sarah felt her heart break. "When my first husband showed up with the Back Alley Killer, I felt betrayed...horribly betrayed. I honestly believed he loved me...and deep down, I believed our broken marriage still had a chance. I wanted to kiss hope again. I was very, very wrong...and it hurt." Sarah looked at the darkness beyond the office window. "Now there's Conrad," she continued. "Conrad is a brave, honest, caring man who is risking his life as we speak to help an old friend. He's faithful to his family and friends."

"Conrad is an okay bloke," Amanda told Sarah and offered her a gentle smile.

Sarah slowly folded her arms for warmth. "Conrad gives

me everything that my first marriage was missing," she told Amanda. "He's what I needed but never had."

"Love, what are you trying to tell me?" Amanda asked.

"Sitting behind this desk is why my first husband stopped loving me," Sarah told Amanda as a painful tear dropped from her eye. "I needed my first husband to love me for who I was...for being a cop, but he never did." Sarah wiped at her tear. "Sitting behind this desk is what Conrad expects of me because he loves me for who I am and respects me as a cop." Sarah pointed to the office window. "I'm far away from Los Angeles, but the old me, the me I thought was gone forever, has found her way back into my heart." Sarah narrowed her eyes. "A man is dead, and I'm going to capture his killer and prevent three harmless old ladies from going to prison."

Amanda studied Sarah's eyes and saw an old fire suddenly blaze up. The old Sarah Garland, who was now Mrs. Spencer, was back. "And I don't have to lose you," Amanda smiled. "You don't have to leave Snow Falls to do any of that."

"Snow Falls is my home, June Bug. A part of me will always live in Los Angeles, but my heart is with you, and with Conrad...here in Snow Falls." Sarah gave Amanda a loving smile. "You've always stood by me and I will always stand by you."

"You're going to make me cry," Amanda promised and wiped a tear away.

"Don't cry, June Bug, because we have a killer to catch." Sarah picked up her cheeseburger and took a small bite. "I'm not sure how. This storm is going to be a real problem for us...and our killer."

"Maybe our killer is hiding out at grandma's house, pretending to pay a visit?" Amanda joked. "There's no better way for a wolf to spend a storm than eating grandma's fresh baked cookies."

Sarah froze. "What did you say, June Bug?" she asked.

"Oh, I was simply joking about our killer hiding out at grandma's house," Amanda explained. "Don't take me seriously, Los Angeles. I'm very exhausted."

"And very brilliant," Sarah exclaimed and jumped to her feet. "Dr. Milton woke up in the bed of his truck. When he looked around, he noticed he was right in town. And the killer...I noticed he ran in a way that seemed to imply he knew his way around. And...why would he return and cut the phone lines in this storm if he didn't have a place nearby to return to safely?"

"The O'Healey sisters live close to town," Amanda gasped. "Los Angeles, I am brilliant. Oh, my hubby would be so proud...if he can ever drag himself home from London."

Sarah ran to Amanda and hugged her. "I'm going to buy you ten dresses," she promised.

"Well...okay," Amanda blushed. "If you insist."

Sarah let go of Amanda and began pacing around the office. "Okay, so we have an idea where our killer might be hiding. The only problem is this storm. I wouldn't dare walk ten feet outside."

"We wouldn't make it ten seconds," Amanda agreed. "It was nearly impossible walking to the phone box."

Sarah felt frustration mocking her. "We're so close," she exclaimed and looked out the window. "There has to be a way."

"If you go out into this storm, you will die."

Sarah spun around and saw Dr. Milton standing in the office doorway. "Dr. Milton, you should be resting."

Dr. Milton stumbled wearily into the office and sat down behind Conrad's desk. "Mrs. Spencer, I can't let you go outside. Please, be reasonable and don't force me to take drastic action. I can't allow you to kill yourself. Conrad would never forgive me…"

"Don't worry," Sarah promised, "Amanda and I have no intention of going outside."

"Good," Dr. Milton said in a relieved voice and pointed at the bags from the diner scattered about. "May I have something to eat, please? I haven't eaten all day and my blood sugar is dropping."

"Oh, of course," Amanda said and fished out a cheeseburger meal for Dr. Milton. She passed the meal to the hungry man and opened the to-go box for him. "It may be a little on the cold side."

"I'm very grateful for any food," Dr. Milton promised. "May I have a cup of coffee, too? I need my strength."

"Aren't you going to rest?" Amanda asked, worried.

Dr. Milton nodded. "Later," he assured Amanda. "I've tried to rest but my mind is far too worried. Not to mention my stomach won't let me sleep when it's empty and rumbling. I'm just grateful my wife is visiting her sister in Nebraska. If my wife were home, she would be out in the storm searching for me as we speak."

"True love," Amanda sighed.

"True love is years of marriage between two people committed to the same purpose," Dr. Milton agreed. "People believe true love is like it is in songs, poems, movies and other nonsense. True love is found in the hearts of those who create an everlasting life together and stick together through the good and the bad. True love is not warm, fuzzy butterflies and…"

Dr. Milton stopped talking for a second. "I've talked more today than I have all month."

"We enjoy hearing you talk," Sarah smiled at Dr. Milton. "It seems to me that you keep a great deal bottled up inside of your heart."

"A man's problems are meant to be handled privately," Dr. Milton replied.

Sarah walked over to Dr. Milton and touched his shoulder. "True friends have strong enough shoulders to help bear each other's burdens."

"That's right," Amanda beamed and carefully checked the back of Dr. Milton's head. Dr. Milton flinched away from her touch and then allowed her to check him. "Doesn't look too bad," she said, exploring the lump of bruising around the wound, "but you're going to be hurting for a while, I'm afraid."

"Yes...Doctor Amanda," Dr. Milton struggled to smile. He looked up into Sarah and Amanda's caring faces and realized that he had been acting like a jerk toward two women who were very special. "I guess Snow Falls is better because of the two of you," he said and looked down at his hands. "Please forgive me for acting so awful toward you. Sarah and Amanda, I'm truly sorry."

"Oh, he called us by our first names...he does love us," Amanda shouted and hugged Dr. Milton's neck. "I knew you loved us all along, you old grouch."

Sarah joined Amanda and hugged Dr. Milton. "You do care," she laughed and kissed Dr. Milton's check.

Dr. Milton felt his cheeks burn red. "Uh...ladies...mind your manners. I am your doctor after all."

Sarah let go of Dr. Milton and smiled. "Yes, you—" she began to say and then stopped.

"What?" Amanda asked.

"Of course!" Sarah yelled and ran out of the office. "Of course, that's it!"

Amanda shrugged her shoulders at Dr. Milton. "My friend might be going insane," she said and chased after Sarah, wondering what in the world the woman was yelling about. Dr. Milton simply shrugged and enjoyed his lukewarm cheeseburger and coffee, feeling pleasantly comfortable in his chair in the quiet office while the two ladies bustled around somewhere in the station building.

Not too far away, Jenson O'Healey also sat feeling pleasantly comfortable, but in a warm kitchen sipping hot coffee with three sweet old ladies who cooed and doted over his every word. Their darling grandson, of course, could do no wrong. "More cookies, dear?" said his aunt, passing him a freshly baked oatmeal raisin cookie. He only gave a half-smile and devoured it in one bite, glancing out at the storm howling ever fiercer around the little cabin.

Chapter Thirteen

Sarah rushed into Andrew's office and ran to a map hanging on the wall. "This is it," she said in an urgent voice.

Amanda made her way to Sarah's side and locked her eyes on the map. "Love, this is a map of the county. Correct me if I'm wrong, but we already know almost every road by heart."

"It's not the roads that I'm interested in," Sarah explained and tapped the map with her finger. "I'm interested in the sewer system that runs through town."

"Sewer system?" Amanda gulped.

"Years back there was a group of bank robbers that used the sewer system to rob banks."

"How?" Amanda asked.

"Certain tunnels ran under the banks," Sarah explained. "The bank robbers would follow the tunnel under the bank and dig into the bank vault from there. They were never caught."

"My goodness," Amanda gasped.

"They got away with millions," Sarah nodded and focused

back on the map. "The O'Healey sisters live within city limits, which means they are on city water and sewage."

"Oh love, please tell me you're not suggesting what I'm thinking," Amanda begged. "Oh please...oh please...oh please."

"June Bug, we can't go out into the storm...not far, anyway. The storm has rendered above-ground travel impossible. But we can travel underground." Sarah looked at her weary friend with a brave smile. "Pete and I chased a killer...a useless drug dealer who killed a buyer...through a sewer system once. We caught them right as they were trying to scurry topside through a manhole cover."

"Love, this is Snow Falls, not Los Angeles," Amanda pointed out. "The tunnels running under the town probably aren't big enough to allow a mouse to crawl through, let alone a human."

"Only one way to find out," Sarah responded. She locked her eyes on the map and pointed to a set of red lines paralleling certain city streets. "According to this map, these represent the sewer tunnels...so let's see...one of the tunnels...runs right behind the station..." Sarah rubbed her chin. "Right behind the station...not bad," she said and focused back on the map. "Now...the O'Healey sisters live...right about here." Sarah pointed to a street on the map.

Amanda leaned forward and then gulped. "A sewer tunnel runs right under the street those old ladies live on."

Sarah nodded. "If we follow this map, we'll be able to travel right to their street."

"If," Amanda moaned and dropped her head. "Love, I like open skies and fresh air. I'm not a mole person."

"Neither am I," Sarah replied. "But, June Bug, I'm a cop and I have a job to do. Jenson O'Healey very well could be at that house. I can't risk waiting until morning to find out." Sarah pointed out the office window. "Jenson probably thinks this storm has us trapped. Right now, he's probably feeling secure...at least until morning. What if morning comes and he turns on his grandmother and his aunts? We have to act."

Amanda moaned again. "I hate it when you make sense," she told Sarah and then simply nodded. "Okay, love, let's go see if we can fit into a sewer tunnel and get all smelly."

Sarah hesitated. "June Bug, you don't have to—"

"If you say I don't have to come I'll make you buy me twenty dresses," Amanda threatened Sarah. "We're a team, love, for better or worse."

"You're something," Sarah smiled and grabbed Amanda's hand, then they ran back to Conrad's office. "Dr. Milton," she said, "Amanda and I have found a way to travel in the storm."

"Underground," Amanda explained in a reluctant voice.

"Using the sewer tunnels, to be exact," Sarah finished. "We believe the killer is at the O'Healeys' and we need to act."

Dr. Milton put down his cheeseburger. "The sewer systems?" he asked, surprised.

"Yes," Sarah confirmed.

"If the tunnels are big enough to let us crawl through," Amanda pointed out.

"Walk through is more like it," Dr. Milton said in an incredulous voice. "Why, a number of years ago I had to go down into the tunnels to tend to a man who fell during pipe work and knocked himself unconscious." Dr. Milton carefully touched the back of his head. "If the wrong size pipes hadn't been ordered, the poor man might not have harmed himself."

"Wrong pipes?"

Dr. Milton nodded and actually chuckled. "The state

ordered the town to replace the old sewer pipes. The old pipes...weren't that old but were cheaply made...and all in horrible condition. So our mayor, always the penny pincher, ordered new pipes. Thought he got himself a good deal." He shook his head in amusement. "He got a good deal because there was a mistake...no one really knows why, but the manufacturer was unloading pipes that were about ten times bigger than we planned to install. The pipes that arrived were large enough for a truck to drive through! The mayor, never one to lose money on a good deal, demanded the new pipes be used. After all, we already had the backhoe. What's another ten feet of digging? At the time most of our roads were still gravel. So, the roads were dug up, one by one, and the pipes were placed down, one by one. Our city pipes have itty-bitty streams running through them, even when the snowmelt comes."

"Thank goodness for mistakes," Sarah smiled. Amanda nodded.

Dr. Milton rubbed his chin. "I suppose the pipes would allow you safe travel," he agreed.

"Very smelly travel," Amanda complained.

"Safety is better than danger," Dr. Milton pointed out.

"I know," Amanda sighed and grabbed her coat. "Okay, love, let's go."

Sarah donned her coat, hat and gloves. "Dr. Milton, I don't know when we'll be back. You're going to have to be in charge, though I doubt anyone will call. Is that okay?"

"Sarah," Dr. Milton replied in a sincere voice, "a man tried to kill me today. My death will destroy my wife...unless it's through old age. Whoever this evil creature is, I want him caught and arrested. I'll manage this end of town. You just do your job." Dr. Milton carefully put his hand on Sarah's shoulder. "You have a very strong reputation and now I understand why. Be careful...the both of you."

Sarah looked into Dr. Milton's eyes and saw a caring man that she wanted to become family with. "We will," she promised and checked her gun. "June Bug, you're going to need a gun."

"I was afraid you were going to say that."

Sarah opened the bottom drawer of Conrad's desk and pulled out a small revolver. "Conrad always keeps this gun here as a backup. Let's just hope you don't have to use it," she said and stuffed the gun into Amanda's coat pocket. "Ready?"

"Ready to be smelly, boss," Amanda tried to joke and looked at Dr. Milton. "Next time tell our mayor to order heated underground tunnels and leave the sewage out of the picture."

"Our mayor is too cheap to listen to reason," Dr. Milton complained.

Sarah smiled, grabbed Amanda's hand, and walked her to the back door. Dr. Milton followed. "Okay, June Bug, the manhole cover leading down into the tunnels is supposed to be right outside the back door. We're going to have to dig around in the snow a bit to find it. Are you okay with that?"

"Do I have a choice?" Amanda sighed.

"Guess not," Sarah said and focused on Dr. Milton. "Dr. Milton, keep the back door open until we're safely down in the tunnel. We're going to need light."

"And this," Dr. Milton said and handed Sarah a snow shovel leaning against the wall near the door.

"And this," Sarah agreed, taking the snow shovel and patting the container of Ice Melt she planned to sprinkle on the manhole to keep it from freezing shut. She went silent for a second, looked into Amanda's face, saw a very brave woman, and nodded. "When this case is solved," she promised, "we'll dress in the prettiest dresses we own, put on the most expensive perfume, wear the brightest jewels, put our hair up and…go eat at the diner." She giggled at the absurd idea.

"Love," Amanda said and patted Sarah on her shoulder, "after this you're driving me to Anchorage for a shopping trip. Maybe even Vancouver British Columbia."

"Fair enough." Sarah looked at Dr. Milton. "We're ready."

Dr. Milton wished Sarah and Amanda well and cracked the back door. As soon as the back door was opened, the powerful winds immediately attacked, followed by blinding snow. "Hurry," Dr. Milton yelled. "The winds will steal your body heat in a matter of minutes."

Sarah didn't waste a second. She threw her left arm over her face and fought her way out into the storm. Amanda made a brave face, saluted Dr. Milton, and followed after Sarah. "Where do we start digging?" she yelled.

Sarah looked to her left and then to her right. The wind and snow were blinding. "You start digging right here," she hollered and pointed down at the snow. "I'll get on my knees and start feeling under the snow."

"I'll feel under the snow…you dig!" Amanda hollered back, unable to even see where to grab the shovel from Sarah.

"Okay!"

Amanda dropped down onto her knees, plunged her hands under the snow, and began feeling around for a manhole cover. "We should be standing on the back sidewalk!"

"We should be," Sarah yelled and began digging at the snow. Dr. Milton carefully kept his eyes on the two brave women, checking his watch every few seconds. "Anything?" Sarah yelled as the icy winds stole her body heat with hungry teeth.

"All I feel is snow," Amanda hollered, feeling her fingers turn to ice. "This isn't working! We're going to freeze!"

"Keep trying...we can't give up!" Sarah begged as she continued to dig through the snow. Finally, she abandoned the snow shovel, dropped down onto her knees, and began digging through the snow. "The manhole cover has to be close...I've seen it before...we should be standing right on it!"

Amanda continued to search the snow. "Los Angeles, we're going to freeze!" she screamed. "I can't even see my own hands...the snow is too blinding...the wind is cutting my face in half and...hey...hey!" Amanda yelled, feeling her gloved hands strike something metal. "Get your shovel!"

Sarah grabbed her shovel and began to frantically dig through the snow. "You found it, June Bug!" she triumphantly hollered. They both shook in fear and relief in the dark, swirling snow.

Dr. Milton stepped out to give them a crowbar he had found in the storage room. "You're going to need this!" he yelled.

Sarah turned around and saw Dr. Milton holding a crowbar with his bare hands. "Your hands," she hollered and quickly took the crowbar. "Get back inside!"

Dr. Milton nodded and hurried back inside. Amanda reached up and took the crowbar from Sarah. "Keep digging, love. We don't have time."

Sarah went back to digging. It seemed for every shovel of snow she threw to the side, the wind blew two more down on top of them. Her arms began to cry out in pain, growing weaker and weaker. And just when Sarah thought she was whipped, the snow shovel struck metal. "There!" she yelled, out of breath.

Amanda began clearing the remaining snow off the manhole cover with her left hand in its bulky glove while Sarah sprinkled the Ice Melt all around the metal surface. When the snow was clear, she started to feel for a hole to stick the crowbar in. "Come on...I've seen this done in the movies," she whispered through chattering teeth as ice began to form on her lashes and eyebrows.

Sarah threw the snow shovel down and began to help Amanda. "Here!" she yelled, "here's a hole. Put the crowbar here!"

"Okay!" Amanda yelled back in an excited voice. She jammed the end of the crowbar into the hole Sarah had found and then froze. "Now what?" she cried.

"Give me the crowbar!" Sarah yelled over the howling winds. Amanda relinquished the handle of the tool to Sarah with a guilty look. Sarah closed her eyes, and then, with all of her strength, let out a mighty cry. "Up and over...get off...move..." she cried, using every muscle in her body to pry the manhole cover free.

"Hey!" Amanda shouted, "love, it's moving...you're doing it...there...it's almost off!"

Sarah let out one last cry and managed to lever the manhole cover free. "There!" she yelled and threw the crowbar down and pulled a flashlight out of her pocket. Amanda followed suit. "Okay, June Bug, let's get underground before we freeze!"

Amanda leaned over the dark hole in the ground, turned on her flashlight, and tossed the beam down into a large tunnel that was indeed, to her shock, big enough to drive a truck through. "There," she hollered and pointed at a set of metal climbing bars embedded in the pipe's concrete. "And...oh my...what a smell!"

"No time to worry about the smell," Sarah yelled. "At least we won't freeze to death." She slid her body into the hole and carefully managed to grip her boots onto one of the metal climbing bars. "We have a killer to catch, June Bug. Let's go."

Amanda watched Sarah vanish into the dark hole like a brave warrior rushing into battle. "We have a killer to catch...if only the way there wasn't all stinky," she moaned and then bravely climbed into the dark hole. As soon as her head vanished, Dr. Milton closed the back door and began praying.

"I've got you," Sarah called up to Amanda and helped her friend down the last few rungs of the ladder. "Easy does it...there you go."

Amanda stepped off the last rung and her left boot landed in a stream of raw sewage. "Oh...I'm going to be sick," she cried and threw her hands over her mouth. "My poor boots!"

"It is foul," Sarah agreed, holding her left hand over her own mouth. "Let's not stand around. Come on."

"Are you sure you know the way?"

"According to the map, this tunnel connects to the pipe running down the street the O'Healeys live on," Sarah explained, fighting back the urge to vomit. "This isn't one of my better ideas, is it?"

"No, it isn't," Amanda agreed.

Sarah aimed her flashlight to her right and studied the tunnel. The vast stretches of the tunnel loomed on either side of them, smelly and slippery with icy trickles of sewage and water, and still very cold...but navigable. Most importantly, it was out of the White Killer storm. "Let's go, June Bug. The sooner we're out in the cold air, the better."

Amanda grabbed the back of Sarah's coat and followed her friend through the tunnel as they worked their way through the sewage, trying to walk to the side whenever possible. Amanda didn't say a word as they walked a long distance, then Sarah stopped and aimed her light up a manhole cover. "Is this it?" asked Amanda.

"Yeah. And look," Sarah said and threw her flashlight at the side of the tunnel. "Each pipe has a street name labeled near the manhole covers. According to that street name, we should be right under the street the O'Healey sisters live on."

"Then let's get out of here before I lose everything I've eaten today," Amanda begged.

"I'm with you," Sarah replied and hurried up a set of metal rungs and began pushing at the manhole cover. "The snow...is making it...heavy...but if I keep pushing..." Sarah stopped, tossed her flashlight down to Amanda, and began fighting with both hands. She had not reckoned on the weight of the storm's snow on top of the manhole cover. Finally, the heavy metal circle began to grind and shift above them. To Amanda's relief, snow began falling down onto her face. "Almost...there...got it!" Sarah grunted out and managed to push the manhole cover far enough to the side to allow them room to squeeze out and escape. She drew in an exhausted breath before she eased her head up into the storm. "Remind me to take a vacation after this."

"What do you see?" Amanda asked in an urgent voice.

"The O'Healey sisters' cabin with lots of lights on," Sarah replied and, without wasting a second, crawled out into the storm. "Come on!" she yelled down to Amanda. "We have a killer to catch!"

Amanda shoved the flashlight into her pocket, hurried up the last few metal rungs, and exploded out into the storm. "Oh…sweet, fresh air…fresh, icy air…come to momma before you turn mean," she whispered and raised her face up at the stormy sky. "Clean my lungs…"

As Amanda drew in fresh air, Sarah pulled out her gun and studied the deluxe cabin shining out into the dark storm with windows full of warm lights. "Time to be a cop," she said, feeling pride enter her heart and adrenaline animate her limbs. "This is for you, honey," she promised Conrad and began fighting her way through the storm drifts, one brave step at a time.

Chapter Fourteen

The brutal winds nearly knocked Amanda down to the ground. She could barely see her hand shading her own eyes from the snow that felt like broken glass digging into her skin, even through her gloves. The lights glowing in the cabin looked like blurry dots far beyond reach. "Are we there yet?" she cried out.

"Almost," Sarah called back, holding Amanda's other hand as tightly as possible and feeling the wind stealing her body heat with every passing second. "We're going to move around to the side of the cabin and look through a window."

Amanda groaned. "I'm frozen solid, love," she yelled, struggling through knee-deep snow. "I don't think I can last much longer, so we better hurry."

Sarah navigated past a tall tree, worked her way to the side of the cabin, and paused at a window. Reluctantly, she let go of Amanda's hand, placed her own hands to the window, and peered into a bright and warm kitchen. It took a second for her eyes to adjust to the light, but when they did, she spotted Jenson O'Healey sitting at a kitchen table drinking coffee and eating a bowl of soup. Abigail was with him. "He's in there," she whispered and quickly turned to Amanda. "Jenson is inside," she said over the winds. "Go to the back door and start knocking as loud as you can. Don't stop until someone answers the door. Make sure you yell 'Police' as loud as you can...over and over and over."

"I'll try," Amanda promised through shivering teeth. "My eyelashes feel like they're freezing stiff...I've never been so cold in all of my life."

"Hang tough," Sarah begged. "I'm going to the front door to wait for Jenson to run." Sarah checked her gun and nodded. "Make sure you yell 'Police' as loud as you can, June Bug. I need you to make Jenson run right into my trap."

Amanda slapped ice off her eyebrows with her gloved fingers. "I'll...try," she promised and looked toward the back of the cabin. "I can barely see...but...we're a team." And with those words, feeling like an iceberg floating in a frozen, white sea, Amanda tucked her head down and began trudging toward the back door. Sarah, feeling like an iceberg herself, turned her face into the howling winds and fought her way toward the front of the cabin.

"Why me?" Amanda moaned in misery as she took one painful, frozen step after another through the deep snow. "Alaska, my hubby said...the land of untamed beauty...Sure, Alaska is beautiful...and I do love the snow...but oh, this storm...will be...the death of me." Amanda rounded the back of the cabin and spotted a light glowing over the back door. "Almost there...keep moving...be tough...think of pretty dresses and pretty hats...warm days...pretty dresses...pretty hats...warm days," she whispered through chattering teeth. "Almost there...back door in reach...keep your eyes shielded...pretty dresses...hot coffee...why me...pretty dresses..." Amanda dared to raise her eyes and was shocked to find that she was standing right at the back door. "I did it," she exclaimed, feeling hope enter her heart.

Without wasting a second, she knocked more ice off her hair and eyebrows and began beating on the back door with both her gloved hands clenched into fists. "Open up!" she hollered at the top of her lungs in a deep voice, "it's the police...open up! Police! Open up. Can you hear me in there? This is the police. Police! Open up…open up!"

Jenson heard Amanda pounding on the door. Then he heard the words "Police! Open up" spill into the kitchen, faint but audible. He jumped up from the kitchen table like a child fleeing a monster lurking in a dark closet, spilled his coffee and knocked the bowl of soup Abigail had prepared for him all over the kitchen floor.

"Jenson!" Abigail cried out in shock, "what in the world has gotten into you? It's only my good friends. They've probably come by to check on me because of the storm."

Jenson, who acted tough and intimidating only when he could bully innocent people or hurt someone without being harmed himself, snatched a black coat off the nearby wooden coat rack and threw it on. "Listen, old lady," he growled through gritted teeth, abandoning the nice grandson act, "I was never here, do you hear me?"

Abigail stared at Jenson in shock. Her loving grandson had suddenly turned into a frightening monster that sickened her —and scared her. "Jenson, what on earth—"

"I wasn't here, old lady," Jenson snapped and bolted out of the kitchen and made his way toward the front door.

"Oh dear," Abigail said in a shaky voice. She stood up,

hurried to the back door, unlocked it, and pulled the door open. Amanda quickly stumbled inside and nearly collapsed. "Oh my," Abigail cried and forced the back door closed against the winds.

"Need to...sit down," Amanda begged through a frozen-stiff jaw and chattering teeth.

Abigail grabbed Amanda's elbow and helped her over to the kitchen table. Amanda stepped in the spilled soup and nearly slipped but managed to sit down in a chair. "I'm so sorry about the mess. My grandson..." Abigail began to speak but stopped as tears began falling from her eyes. "Oh my..."

Amanda grabbed Abigail's hands. "Sarah will bring him back," she promised and then shot to her feet, remembering. "Have to help my girl...sit tight."

Outside in the snow, Sarah positioned herself on a snow-covered front porch. She dropped down onto one knee, aimed her gun at the front door, and waited. "Come on out," she dared Jenson in a muttered whisper, trying to ignore the cold. To her delight, seconds later, Jenson obeyed. The front door jerked open and Jenson appeared, frantic to escape. He didn't spot Sarah. His eyes were locked on the dark night. "Freeze!" Sarah yelled and fired a warning shot up into the air. The bullet struck the roof of the porch and worked its way through, loosening a small avalanche of snow onto their heads before it rocketed away into the storm.

"Don't shoot!" Jenson cried out in confusion, covered in a dumping of snow. He threw his hands up into the air. "Don't kill me...please!" He blinked madly, unable to see.

Sarah bolted up and aimed her gun right at Jenson's chest. "Back inside, move!"

Jenson backed up to the front door and then, out of a mad

desperation, pawed the snow away from his face and tried to run at the last minute. He was greeted by Amanda.

"I don't think so, you filthy monster," Amanda growled and aimed her gun at Jenson's face. "I can't miss from this distance."

Jenson froze, staring at the gun, and tried his best not to wet himself. The suave intellect with wavy black hair and good looks saw his plans destroyed and the law closing in, and he caved like the coward and fake that he was. "Don't kill me," he begged. "Oh please, don't kill me."

Sarah guided him back inside, with Amanda backing her up. Sarah stepped inside the foyer and slammed the front door closed. Even though she was frozen solid and her body was crying out in pain, she managed to stay on her feet and remain in full control. "Lie down on the floor, on your belly, like the coward you are, with your hands behind your back." Jenson quickly obeyed. Sarah handed Amanda her gun, pulled a pair of handcuffs out of her coat pocket, and slapped them on Jenson. "Alright, on your feet."

Jenson crawled back to his feet, which wasn't easy. His knees trembled and his eyes darted around the room in terror and confusion, unsure of what to do. He looked at Sarah and Amanda, wondering how two small-town, backwoods lady cops had outsmarted him. While wearing dresses, nonetheless. The storm, he thought, should have kept the entire police department under lockdown. But there was no sense crying over spilt milk, Jenson told himself. He had to figure out a way to escape. "What is this...what is this all about?" he asked, playing up his tremors of cold as if they were genuine terror, wanting to appear as much a victim as possible.

"Murder," Sarah said, spotting Abigail peeking her head

into the foyer. The poor woman looked absolutely distraught. The situation was no longer exciting like a television episode. "Abigail, honey, go back to the kitchen."

Abigail ignored Sarah, however. She eased into the foyer and walked up to Jenson, who stood cowering in the corner of her immaculate living room, dripping snow and filth all over the carpet. "Why?" she demanded in a tremulous, hurt tone. "Mitchel Cochran is dead. The feud is over. Why?"

"The gold," Jenson hissed without a moment of remorse. "I want the gold. Just like everyone else."

Abigail sighed. "The gold is cursed," she said and tried to touch Jenson's arm. Jenson yanked away. "Oh, your papa would be so upset with you, Jenson. He worked so hard to give you such a good life."

"You stupid old biddy," Jenson snapped, "my papa, your darling son, was involved all along. He's not the golden boy you think he is."

Abigail frowned. "I know my sweet Caleb is a troubled soul," she admitted and looked at Sarah. "A mother hates to acknowledge the darker truths about her children. A mother will always take delight in her own son, even when she knows the truth." Abigail looked down at her wrinkled hands. "I know my son had a drinking problem...for many years. He has a troubled heart...but there is goodness in him, and I take joy in knowing that." Abigail raised her eyes. "I will not tolerate you bad-mouthing your father, Jenson. Besides, a woman has to live her own life," she told him with a dignified look around the neat little cabin living room. "I have lived a long and beautiful life, and my sisters and I ended the feud. That was our gift to all of our loved ones. Today was supposed to be such a wonderful day..."

Sarah heard movement. She turned her head and saw Betty and Martha appear, both dressed in lovely though faded evening gowns that reminded Sarah of the nineteen-thirties. "What is happening?" Betty asked in a worried voice.

"Yes, indeed, tell us," Martha pleaded with Abigail. Both looked terribly distressed to see Jenson handcuffed and dripping with filthy snow.

Sarah took her gun and placed it back in the ankle holster. "Ladies," she began to speak but then stopped and sniffed the air. The smell of three different, powerful perfumes entered her nose. "The poison!" she yelled and grabbed Jenson, swung him around, and stared him straight in the eyes. "You were going to kill them, weren't you?"

Jenson cast his gaze down at the floor. "I don't know what you're—"

Sarah dug her hands into the pockets of Jenson's coat and began digging around. "Aha," she said and pulled out a small, fancy bottle of perfume. "Why do you have my perfume?" Abigail asked in confusion.

Sarah tossed the perfume bottle to Amanda and pulled a glass tube full of red liquid out of Jenson's right coat pocket. "This must be the poison."

"I...don't understand," Abigail confessed. She looked at Jenson with confusion. "Jenson, please, tell me what this is all about."

Jenson kept his eyes low. He was surely busted but he wasn't about to let his tongue run loose. "I want to speak to my attorney."

Sarah shook her head in disgust. "Abigail, honey, before I tell you what's happening, please, tell me one thing. Tell me how you think you killed Mitchel Cochran," she begged.

"Please, love," Amanda pleaded with Abigail.

Abigail looked at her sisters with reluctance and understanding. "Maybe the time has arrived for us to...reconsider our desire to remain silent?"

Betty and Martha stared at each other and then slowly nodded their heads. "Indeed, it has," they agreed and looked at Sarah. "We fear we have been very foolish."

"Not foolish," Sarah promised. "Just cautious. Now please, talk to me."

Abigail motioned for her sisters to join them in the roomy living room beautifully decorated with antique furnishings that could make a person's heart melt. Sarah grabbed Jenson's arm and stationed him on the entry way tiles so he wouldn't make a mess and fastened his handcuffs to a radiator temporarily. He could see and hear them, but he could not budge.

Abigail strolled over to a stone fireplace with its roaring fire and warmed her old hands. "We knew the time had come for Mitchel Cochran to die," she told Sarah in a low voice.

"We had waited much too long to begin with," Betty added.

"Indeed, we did," Martha agreed.

"We wanted to kill Mitchel Cochran many years ago, but we could not," Abigail continued.

"Why?" Sarah confessed.

Betty and Martha walked over to a pink and white settee and sat primly. "It's all about the feud," Martha confessed, and Betty murmured in agreement.

"Indeed, it is," Abigail nodded. She turned to Sarah, slowly beginning to warm up by the fire's warmth, and then walked her eyes to Jenson. "It was always said that Stephen Greenlight killed Billy Cochran."

"Yeah, I know," Jenson snapped.

"Mind your manners," Sarah warned Jenson. Jenson saw that the woman was prepared to fill him full of bullets and looked down at the floor.

Abigail, unable to look at her grandson any longer, turned back to the fire. "The truth is...my sisters and I killed Billy Cochran...by mistake."

"Oh yes, a mistake indeed," Betty agreed.

"A horrible mistake," Martha nodded.

"My sisters and I were very young," Abigail continued. "We so loved Stephen and were delighted when our Papa agreed to a visit. It was spring, and after a long winter Papa knew us girls needed to catch our breath. So he packed us up, along with Mother, and we traveled to this area. Oh, Stephen was so excited to see us—"

"But not Miren...that awful, awful woman," Betty added.

"Awful indeed," Martha agreed with a sorrowful nod.

"Miren went and told Billy Cochran that my Papa had arrived for a visit. Billy Cochran was furious and threatened to kill Papa unless he left. Papa refused. Billy Cochran gave Papa until the next day to leave—"

"And promised to shoot Papa if we stayed," Betty told Sarah.

"That awful man meant his words, too," Martha added. "We girls became very scared for Papa."

"Indeed, we did," Betty agreed. "Papa was a brave man, but he wasn't very fast with a rifle. Everyone knew Billy Cochran could outdraw and outshoot Papa."

"Yet poor Papa refused to leave," Martha continued.

"And so, we girls," Abigail picked up, "decided to take matters into our own hands. When night fell, we snuck away from the Greenlight cabin after everyone had fallen asleep and we handled things."

"Indeed, we did," Betty nodded.

"For Papa, of course," Martha added. "We loved our Papa very much and couldn't let him die."

Sarah looked at Amanda. "Sit down, June Bug. We're in for a long story."

Amanda looked down at her boots, wrinkled her nose, and sat down next to Betty and Martha and waited for the story to begin as the storm howled and raged outside. "At least we're inside," she said in a grateful voice. "Now all we need is popcorn and a hot coffee."

Chapter Fifteen

Sarah closed her eyes and listened to Abigail begin her story. She shut out the world and awakened the writer inside her heart, bringing the story to life in her mind just as she did when she sat down at her own typewriter.

It was a dark and cool night, Abigail told them, *as three young girls bravely escaped into the dark wilderness of an untamed land. The girls, desperate to save their Papa, aimed their sights on the camp of a horrible man determined to cause death and misery to their family. "Careful now," the oldest of the girls, Abigail, whispered to her sisters. "We mustn't be heard or seen."*

"Papa will be very mad at us if he finds out," the second sister, Betty, whispered.

"Oh, simply furious," the youngest sister, Martha, agreed as they crept past the tall, dew-soaked trees that appeared older than time.

Abigail, more familiar with the wilderness, followed a moonlight-bathed path toward the camp of her Papa's enemy. She understood the wilderness—the dangers and the beauty—and knew how to respect the land her bare feet walked upon. "We're going to steal that awful man's rifle and throw it in the lake and then go back home safe to our beds."

"If that mean man doesn't have his rifle, he can't shoot Papa, right?" Betty whispered.

Abigail assured her sisters the plan would work. They continued to follow the path, walking under a full moon, until Abigail led them to a clearing. In the clearing, she spotted a small, dark cabin. "We have walked a very long ways," she said. "But we made it. There's Billy Cochran's cabin."

Betty and Martha peeked at the cabin through the early spring underbrush and became very scared. "How are we going to steal that awful man's rifle?" they asked as owls began to speak overhead, hidden in the trees.

"We'll sneak through the front door," Abigail explained in an uncertain voice. "Papa keeps his rifle next to the front door...I'm certain most men do."

Betty and Martha looked at each other with worried eyes. What if the door was barred and locked from inside? "We have Papa to think about," the youngest sisters reminded each other and looked back at Abigail with determination. "Let's hurry," they pleaded. The lake was still a good walk from the cabin in the clearing and the bears would surely be hungry after sleeping all winter.

Abigail bravely drew in a deep breath and got her bare feet moving silently down the rocky path. When she came close to the cabin she slowed down, peered all around to search the moonlit night, and then whispered to her sisters: "Billy Cochran lives alone in this cabin. That awful Miren is back at Stephen Greenlight's cabin. If we're quiet, we should be able to steal the rifle without being seen or heard."

"Not seen...not heard," Betty and Martha whispered back and

worriedly followed their big sister up onto the wooden porch. The porch floorboards creaked and whined under their feet. "Walk lightly," Betty whispered in desperation, and they all went up on tiptoes.

"Listen," Abigail said and stopped moving. Betty and Martha froze and listened to the night. The sound of heavy snoring rushed out of the cabin like gravel flung off a cliff. "Billy Cochran is fast asleep...we need to hurry." Abigail gently pushed open the front door to the one-room cabin filled with darkness and the smell of sweat and dirt. In the far corner, her eyes made out the dim shape of a narrow bed. Billy Cochran lay fast asleep, his snoring loud as thunder. "Okay," she whispered, "it's safe."

Betty and Martha nodded their heads and eased into the cabin behind Abigail. Abigail dropped down onto her knees and began feeling around for the rifle. Betty and Martha came up behind her. "The rifle has to be close to the door," she whispered.

Betty, feeling a strange premonition wash over her, raised her eyes and looked at the fireplace. To her horror, she saw the bright moonlight flooding through the open door and reflecting dimly from the rifle's barrel. "Oh no," she whispered urgently to her sister, "the rifle is hanging over the fireplace."

Abigail raised her eyes and spotted the rifle. "I'll get it," she whispered and carefully crawled across the floor to the fireplace.

"Hurry," Betty pleaded.

"Oh, please hurry," Martha added.

Abigail reached the fireplace, stood up, and began reaching for the rifle. Only her arms weren't long enough to reach the rifle. "I need a chair," she said in a tiny whisper.

"Oh my," Betty and Martha gasped. They picked up the old wooden chair from the crooked kitchen table and carried it over to

their sister as Billy Cochran snored away. Abigail positioned the chair in front of the fireplace. "Hurry," her sisters urged.

"I will," Abigail promised and quickly climbed up on the chair. "I can reach it," she whispered.

Betty and Martha watched their sister cautiously take the rifle down off its wooden rack and then prepare to climb down from the chair. As Abigail began to climb down, the barrel of the rifle struck a metal cup hiding in the shadows of the mantle. The metal cup flew off the mantle of the fireplace and crashed down onto the wooden floor with a terrific clatter. "What...who's there!?" Billy Cochran yelled, startled out of a deep sleep. "Who's in my cabin!"

"Run!" Abigail screamed, spotting Billy rising from his bed. She jumped off the chair and began to race toward the front door. Betty and Martha made it out first. "Run!" Abigail yelled again as her feet reached the threshold of the cabin, still clutching the rifle. But before Abigail could make it through the doorway, Billy Cochran grabbed the back of her dress. "No!" Abigail screamed and struggled and finally yanked herself away from Billy as hard as she could. The back of her dress tore loose. Abigail stumbled forward, tripped over her feet, and tumbled down onto the narrow front porch. Her momentum carried her forward and she tumbled right off the porch into the dirt. Abigail felt the rifle fly free from her hands and land on the ground next to her, banging onto a rock. When the rifle struck the hard ground, it came to life and left Abigail nearly deaf for a moment. Then a loud, painful cry split the air.

"You...shot me!" Billy Cochran cried out and stumbled back into his cabin holding his chest. Then, panting and heaving in tremendous pain, he collapsed onto the floor and dropped dead.

"Oh my," Abigail cried in shock. "I didn't mean to...it was a mistake...honest!"

Betty and Martha ran over to their sister, pulled her to her feet, and began to run. As they did, Stephen Greenlight appeared along the path coming toward them. "What are you girls doing out at this time of night?" he demanded, holding a rifle of his own. "I came here to try and talk some sense into that man. What are you doing here? Was that a rifle shot I heard? Tell me none of you are hurt!" His eyes went wider when he saw Abigail's torn nightgown.

Abigail, unable to contain her emotions any longer, burst into tears in Stephen's arms. "I didn't mean to shoot him, honest," she cried. "The rifle went off by mistake...honest."

Stephen put his arms around Abigail and stared at the dark cabin. He was a hard, toughened woodsman but had a gentle way about him when it came to family. "Stay here," he said, letting go of Abigail and walking into Billy Cochran's cabin. Minutes later he came out, picked up Billy Cochran's rifle, and returned to where Abigail and her sisters huddled together on the path. "Billy Cochran is dead," he said in a careful voice.

"We only wanted to steal his rifle and throw it in the lake," Betty cried.

"But he woke up and chased me," Abigail said through tear-filled eyes. "He grabbed my dress...I yanked free so hard that I fell off the porch...the rifle hit the ground and went off all by itself...honest."

"That's the truth," Martha insisted, "We saw the whole thing." She wrapped her arms around Abigail. "We came here to save Papa..."

Stephen stroked his thick beard and looked around. "Okay, girls," he said in a calm voice, "here's the deal. Tonight, we're going to make a pact. No one is to ever know the truth. No one ever needs to know the truth. I'm going to say I killed Billy

Cochran because he stole my gold. Everyone knows that Billy Cochran has been stealing from my claim anyways. I'll say I came to confront him and he drew his rifle on me."

"But there isn't any gold," Abigail insisted.

Stephen leaned Billy's rifle against a tree, bent down, and put his hands on Abigail's shoulders. "Oh yes, there is," he promised. "I have lots and lots of gold. I've been letting Billy steal from a claim that has a little gold on it, but the real claim, girls," Billy smiled, "is loaded. And someday all that gold is going to be all ours. I'm going to share it with all of my family."

"Even that awful Miren?" Abigail dared to ask as she wiped at her tears.

Stephen sighed. "Love makes a man blind...I guess I'm like Samson in the Bible," he said in a miserable voice. "For whatever reason there is, I love her. But listen to me," Stephen added, "after I confess to killing Billy, I have a terrible premonition that woman is going to pack her bags and hit the trail. She never married me for love, girls. I'm a strong man who has a good nose for gold. That's why Miren married me. But..." Stephen looked at the dark cabin and then focused his eyes on the faces of three very scared girls that he loved with all of his heart. "Family comes first. And...who knows? Maybe this is a blessing in disguise. Now, you girls get on back to my cabin and let me take care of business."

Abigail looked at her sisters. "Let's go," she said and quickly hugged Stephen. "We'll never forget you or the sacrifice you are making here tonight for our sake. And we promise...someday, we'll show you how grateful we are," she said and ran off into the bright moonlight with her sisters.

Chapter Sixteen

Sarah emerged from her reverie as Abigail finished her tale and found herself still in the warm living room. "How does Mitchel Cochran play into this?" she asked.

Abigail turned away from the fire. "Miren," she said sorrowfully.

Sarah walked over to the fire and warmed her hands. "I thought Stephen Greenlight set it in his mind to kill Billy Cochran to take back his wife and gold. I was wrong. Tell me what else I need to know to understand."

Abigail sighed. "After Miren found out that Billy had been shot, she became a very bitter woman, but to everyone's surprise, she remained married to Stephen." Abigail looked at her two sisters. "Stephen was blinded by that woman." Abigail looked at Jenson too and then tore her eyes away. "Over time Miren convinced Stephen to allow her brother to come and live with them, a very ugly man by the name of Roger Cochran. Why Stephen agreed to let another Cochran into his life is beyond me. As far as everyone was concerned, with Billy being dead, we believed the feud was over. But we were wrong."

"Very wrong," Betty agreed.

"Very, very wrong," Martha added.

Abigail walked over to a soft reading chair and sat down. "Miren and her brother Roger...they killed our beloved Stephen and stole all of his gold...every last ounce of it and moved to California. Papa would have killed them for such treachery and villainy but by the time the news reached him, it was too late...Miren and Roger Cochran had vanished with Stephen's gold."

"But we never forgot Stephen and what he did for us," Betty promised.

"Indeed, we did not," Martha agreed. "We vowed to find Stephen's gold and bury it next to him."

"Only," Abigail added, "when a woman marries and has children, well, life gets in the way of a promise, dear," she explained to Sarah. "My sisters and I were forced, for many years, to put our promise on hold. It wasn't until our children were grown that we were able to hire a man to help us fulfill our promise."

Sarah looked at Abigail. "Abigail, before we go any further, please, tell me, how did you think you killed Mitchel Cochran? Speak plainly."

"We found Stephen's gold, of course," Abigail stated in a proud voice. "All of Stephen's gold...or what's left of it...it is hidden in one of those...what do you call it?"

"I think it's called a warehouse, dear," Betty told Abigail.

"Indeed," Martha agreed.

Abigail nodded. "We found Stephen's gold in a warehouse," she confirmed. "Once we found it, we had to tell that Mitchel Cochran it was all over. We all knew Mitchel went into town for his morning coffee so we marched into town, told him we found his gold, and as soon as we did, he had a heart attack. Good riddance."

"The shock was too much for that awful man," Betty explained. "The news killed him, and we're proud that he's dead."

"Indeed," Martha added.

Sarah bit down on her lower lip. "Ladies, I'm afraid I have some bad news. You didn't kill Mitchel Cochran. It certainly wasn't your news that did him in," she added. "I don't think Mitchel Cochran wanted Stephen's gold, either. I think he knew the gold was cursed."

"That's right," Amanda jumped in. "We went to his cabin. The man was living like he was the poorest pauper in town. Also, we found a key to a storage unit. If that key leads to a storage unit full of a whole bunch of gold...why would a man lock up his gold in a place where it could be easily looted? Why not use a bank?"

"Because he was a fool," Jenson snapped from his position near the door, struggling against his handcuffs to face them. "Old Mitchel never wanted the gold but refused to tell anyone where it was. His daughters Alicia and Mandy did some digging and realized you three were living in the same town as Mitchel and figured you must know something. That's when they came to me." Jenson made a disgusted face. "We tried to work Mitchel first, but he wouldn't talk."

"Oh my," Abigail gasped.

"Abigail, there's more," Sarah sighed. "Your son Caleb is… involved. Not of his own free will, though." Sarah looked at

Jenson with no pity for his tortured squirming. "Isn't that right?"

"Yeah, yeah," Jenson nodded in embarrassment. "My old man was forced to play the bad guy against his will. I'll give him that much."

"And it seems that he doesn't know the real truth, either," Sarah continued. "Caleb O'Healey isn't aware that you killed Billy Cochran...by accident. He believes the story about the gold causing the heart attack. It seems that everyone else does, too."

Amanda rubbed her chin. "All this over gold...which is nothing more than money," she said in a thoughtful voice. "Sure, I'm a girl that likes the good life, but goodness...is money truly worth all of this to you?" She gave Jenson a hard look. "Look at all the heartache and trouble it has caused."

"Cry me a river," Jenson snapped. "You have no idea how it was for me growing up, trying to be perfect, scraping by with nothing. When Alicia and Mandy showed up, they did me a favor...and Charlie, he showed me what it was like to really live." Jenson sneered at his grandmother Abigail. "My father was a weakling in the end. I enjoyed watching my friends destroy him and break him down into a pile of mush."

Sarah pointed at Jenson. "You sure talk big for someone who's currently handcuffed and facing jail time for murder," she said and sniffed the air. "Who's the pile of mush, here, hmm? And is that the delicious scent of irony I smell in the air?" She gave him a menacing grin.

Jenson stared into Sarah's eyes and lowered his head in shame. It was easy for him to bully an old lady like his grandmother, or to watch his father be tortured into compliance by the harsh words of his friends, but now that everything was out in the open, he didn't have the courage to stand up to a brave woman. "That's more like it," Amanda said, standing up and walking over to Abigail. "Perry Mason is a lot more fun, huh, love?" she asked and hugged Abigail. "Sorry for calling you a crazy old bat."

Abigail hugged Amanda back but didn't say a word. Instead, she stared at Jenson sorrowfully and realized deep inside of her heart that Mitchel Cochran's death had ended something even darker than she had known existed. Both pain and relief washed through her heart. Her own family had betrayed her, though it had all turned out okay in the end.

"Shall we have a little coffee?" Betty asked, uncertain of what to do with their guests, still dripping melted snow in the living room.

"Indeed," Martha agreed, and the two younger sisters hurried away to the kitchen realizing that Perry Mason was fun but real life sure could be, as the young people say, a real bummer.

Chapter Seventeen

Sarah parked outside an apartment building bathed with bright sunlight and eased a pair of dark sunglasses off her face. "This is the place," she told Pete. "If our sources are right, Caleb O'Healey should be inside."

Pete tossed a cigar into his mouth. "We'll sit for a while," he said and leaned his elbow out of the gray SUV Sarah had parked behind a UPS truck.

Sarah turned off the engine and glanced into the back seat. Conrad and Amanda looked up at her. "We'll sit for a while," she announced.

Conrad smiled. "No rush. Sun feels good."

"I bet it does, surfer boy," Amanda teased Conrad and poked at the blue, white and red floral Hawaiian shirt he was wearing. "You look like a spoiled bloody pineapple."

Conrad rolled his eyes and tossed on a pair of sunglasses. "I'm supposed to be a tourist," he said and tossed a thumb at the pink and blue sundress and woven hat Amanda wore.

"And what's with that hat? You planning to use it to fly to London?"

Amanda gasped. "My hat is quite lovely, you twit."

"Okay, you two," Sarah laughed. "We're on a stakeout, not a boxing match."

"Easy for you to say, love," Amanda complained. "You're wearing a regular dress. I'm forced to dress like this bloke's wife and act like a silly tourist."

Pete grinned. He loved it when Conrad and Amanda got after each other. "So tell me," he said, chewing on his cigar, "whatever came of the gold?"

Sarah looked over at Pete, studied the wrinkled gray suit he was wearing, and sighed. She had her old Pete back, and that was worth all the gold in the world to her. "Well," she said, "the O'Healey sisters married three Irish men who knew how to dig for gold themselves. They're loaded," she explained.

"Must be nice," Pete said. "Living on a policeman's pension isn't going to be easy."

Sarah nudged Pete. "I have your back," she promised.

"I know," Pete smiled, "but I don't like handouts. I have some money put away. You can buy my cigars and Chinese food."

"Can we get back to the gold?" Conrad asked, "Before Pete steals my wife?"

"Sure, sure," Pete laughed.

Sarah smiled. "The gold rightfully belonged to the O'Healey sisters...in a way, I guess," she said. "The O'Healey sisters told me they never thought about what to do with the gold after they confronted Mitchel Cochran. Mitchel Cochran never knew the O'Healey sisters were following him wherever he went, even when he left Snow Falls, or so they claim. I guess we'll never know the real mindset of Mitchel Cochran or what he was truly thinking. There's a lot of unanswered questions left in my mind." Sarah picked up a strawberry smoothie and took a sip. "Anyway, the O'Healey sisters decided to give all the gold to a children's cancer center instead of burying it next to Stephen Greenlight."

"How much gold?" Pete asked.

"Millions upon millions, love," Amanda answered from the backseat.

Conrad whistled. "I should have stayed home instead of helping my friend. Convinced those old ladies to let me take some of that gold off their hands."

"Speaking of your friend, how is he?" Sarah asked, keeping a close eye on the apartment building while a warm breeze played in the fronds of the palm trees lining the street.

"He's okay," Conrad answered Sarah. "We caught the bad guys and that's all that matters."

"That's all that matters," Sarah whispered in a proud voice.

"What?" Pete asked and lit his cigar.

"Oh, do you have to do that," Amanda fussed at Pete. "You know how I hate the smell of your cheap cigars."

"This isn't a cheap cigar," Pete barked. "Sarah bought me this cigar as a present. This cigar cost a lot of money."

"A reward for helping me track down Alicia and Mandy Cochran," Sarah smiled.

"And don't forget Charlie Moorington, kiddo," Pete added.

"And Mr. Night Life himself," Sarah agreed.

Conrad leaned back in his seat. "Okay, so you guys caught the bad guys and I guess I have a clear understanding of this case. But what I don't understand is why Jenson O'Healey was going to kill the O'Healey sisters if he believed they knew where the gold was hidden? Wasn't his intention to blackmail them for murder and force them to confess?"

"That was the original plan," Sarah agreed, "but Caleb was able to contact his son and tell him about our talk—he guessed some of what we had planned. Jenson confessed to his father that he switched plans, decided to poison Betty and Martha, and threaten to spray the trigger smell on them unless Abigail spilled the beans. The rat was desperate, Conrad."

"And not very smart," Amanda added. "To be honest, none of the bad guys seemed very smart this time. Greedy and cruel, but not smart."

"That's what happens when you get desperate," Sarah explained and tossed her eyes at the front door of the apartment building. She saw a UPS driver exit the building, run to his truck, jump in and speed away. A couple of minutes later, the front door opened again. Caleb O'Healey peeked his head through, looked around, and then eased out into the sun. "Okay, there he is," Sarah whispered. "Conrad, Amanda, do your thing."

"You got it, honey," Conrad said, leaned forward, kissed Sarah on her cheek, and then carefully left the SUV without being seen by Caleb. Amanda blinked cigar smoke from her eyes, held onto her wide-brimmed sun hat, and followed after Conrad. As soon as she was clear of the SUV, she started to complain. "We're lost and you refuse to ask for directions."

Conrad unfolded a paper "Map to the Stars" and pretended to study it as they sauntered toward Caleb, who was already crossing the street toward them. "I'm not lost...dear," he snapped back. "I know exactly where I am."

Caleb spotted Amanda and Conrad arguing, studied their

clothing, and recognized their type. Tourists, looking for celebrity houses and bits of old California history. Well, they wouldn't rope him into their little marital spat. He continued toward his parked BMW. Even though he was nervous and paranoid, he kept reminding himself that it had been months since he had fled from Anchorage and nothing had happened. "Keep it together. Everything's fine. I'm safe," he whispered and quickly brushed lint off the fancy suit he wore. "New name...new job...I'm safe."

Conrad eased closer to Caleb and then stopped. "Hey mister," he said, lowering his map, "maybe you can help me?"

"I'm sorry. I don't have the time," Caleb said in a quick voice and tried to hurry past Conrad.

"Then maybe you have time for this," Amanda said and pulled a gun out from her red purse. "Walk," she ordered and pointed at the SUV where Sarah and Pete sat waiting.

"Not bad," Conrad congratulated Amanda.

"I told your wife that I could pull this off," Amanda beamed. "Now she has to take me to London to see my hubby."

"Yeah, yeah," Conrad sighed. "You won the bet." He looked at Caleb. Caleb swallowed then tried to run. Conrad grabbed his arm. "We're the police, stupid," he said, "so be smart for once."

"Please," Caleb begged, "I didn't do anything...I didn't hurt anyone. I swear. I was forced to—"

"Shut up and come on," Conrad ordered Caleb and frog-marched the man to the SUV. "Amanda won the bet," he told Sarah. "Looks like you're going to London."

Sarah grinned. "I figured she would win. I've taught her well, honey."

Caleb swallowed. "Please—"

"Get in," Sarah told Caleb in a stern voice. "We're taking a ride."

Conrad shoved Caleb into the backseat. Amanda hurried around the SUV and crawled in beside Caleb so he was trapped between them. "All set, love."

Pete turned around in his seat and looked at Amanda. "Not bad for a rookie. I thought you would flake and need Conrad to cover you."

"What Pete is saying is he owes me ten bucks," Sarah informed Amanda as she pulled away from the apartment building.

"You two bet on me?" Amanda asked and rolled her eyes. "I should have known."

Caleb glanced at Conrad and then looked at Amanda. "Where are you taking me?"

"You'll see," Sarah told Caleb and aimed the SUV toward the deserted beach she and Pete always visited. Fifteen minutes later, she pulled into a sandy parking lot and parked beside a black Lincoln Town car. "Here we are," she said and turned to give her best friend an exasperated look. "Goodness, why do you two have to argue so much? You fussed the entire drive."

"Your darling husband started it," Amanda complained and waved more cigar smoke away from her face. "Pete, love, will you douse the cigar?"

"Nope," Pete grinned and took a puff.

Conrad looked at Amanda. "You started the argument."

"I did not...you...twit," Amanda fired back.

"Oh, for crying out loud...shut up," Caleb begged. "Who cares if he cheats at Scrabble. My life is on the line, you bunch of...morons."

Sarah held back a laugh. "Come on," she told Caleb.

"Where are you taking me to?" Caleb asked in a scared voice, fearing he had been lied to and that the four people holding him were not police at all. As far as he was concerned, he was a hostage about to be taken down to the beach and drowned.

"You'll see," Sarah promised. "Conrad, honey, get our package out of the backseat."

"No funny stuff," Conrad warned Caleb in a tough voice and pulled him out into a warm breezy day by the bright blue-green ocean that was tossing gentle waves onto the lonely beach. "Walk."

Caleb watched Sarah walk over to the black car and slowly followed. "Okay, Abigail," Sarah called out, "he's here."

Caleb froze in horror. "Abigail...my mother?" He panicked and watched the back door of the car open. Abigail appeared, slowly climbed out into the sun, and then smoothed down the lovely blue and white dress she had chosen to wear for the day she would confront her wayward son. "Mother?" Caleb gasped.

Abigail raised her eyes, looked at her son, and fought back tears. "Come over here to me, son," she said in a soft, loving voice.

"You heard the lady," Conrad said and nudged Caleb toward Abigail.

Caleb hesitated and then moved forward on nervous legs. "Mother...it's not what you think...I..."

"Come to your mother," Abigail said as a gentle tear left her eye. She held out her arms. "Come to your mother."

Caleb, seeing his mother begin to cry, broke down, stumbled into Abigail's arms, and began to weep. "I never wanted it to be like this...I swear. I'm so sorry for...betraying you...I put my life before your own...I'm so sorry."

Abigail gently took her right hand and raised Caleb's chin. "In life, dear, there is real gold and fool's gold. The gold we dig up from the earth can be real gold if we use it for good...or it can become fool's gold if we use it unwisely and let it twist us toward evil. The same applies to our hearts. Life can be good if we live it with love...or it can become a fool's errand if we bathe in hate." Abigail forced a tender smile to her face. "These very kind cops are true gold. You should thank them."

Caleb wiped at his tears. "I don't understand."

"Jenson O'Healey confessed to a whole bunch of ugly stuff," Sarah explained. "Alicia and Mandy Cochran played tough for a while but finally broke down after Charlie Moorington betrayed them and tried to make a deal with the Feds. We know that you were forced into playing a bad role in this whole charade, Mr. O'Healey."

"Yes, you were, my sweet son," Abigail said and kissed Caleb's cheek. "Sisters?"

Betty and Martha peeked their heads out of the back seat of the car. "We're going to take you home to Snow Falls with us," said Betty.

"And you're going to rest," added Martha.

"And no funny stuff," Conrad warned Caleb. "Your mother is willing to forgive you and we're willing to help you get a second chance at life. You mess up this time and it's off to prison."

"We've talked with the Feds," Sarah told Caleb. "They've dropped all charges against you and left you to our care. They have the bad guys they want. You're small fry to them."

Caleb couldn't believe his ears. He looked at Abigail in

shock and then, as he stared into his mother's eyes, he realized that his real punishment was much more internal and real than jail could ever be. "I'll never forgive myself," he whispered.

"I'm afraid you've created your own prison," Abigail agreed and then gently touched Caleb's heart. "But a mother's love is neverending and, if you let me, I'll help you escape from your prison and teach you how to find real gold. How to live with love again."

"I would...like that," Caleb told Abigail, dropped down to his knees, put his hands over his face, and began crying. "I would like that very much...very much..."

"This was never on Perry Mason," Betty said in a sad voice.

"Indeed not," Martha agreed and let out a heavy sigh.

"But there is a happy ending," Sara promised and softly kissed Abigail on her cheek. "We'll be around," she promised and then turned to Conrad, Amanda and Pete. "Who wants to take a walk on the beach?"

Conrad took Sarah's hand, gave her a kiss, and said, "I do."

"You two go ahead," Pete said, "I want to stand here and finish my cigar."

"Yeah, go on," Amanda smiled and shooed Sarah and Conrad away, "go be love birds."

Conrad gave Amanda a grateful smile and walked his wife down onto the warm, bright sand of the beach. Sarah looked back over her shoulder, saw Amanda and Pete standing next to a man crying on his knees and an old woman gently touching her son's shoulder, and smiled. "Is this for real?" she asked Conrad, "or am I dreaming? Is...evil going to jump out at me at any second and ruin this moment?" She thought of the spectral snowman who seemed to haunt her thoughts amidst the worst cases, but at the moment, those visions seemed as far away as the moon.

Conrad stopped walking, took Sarah into his arms, held her tight, and whispered, "This is real. Our story is forever," he promised. "And if that snowman comes back, we'll fight it together as one."

"One heart," Sarah said, placing her hand over Conrad's heart with a smile. And with those words, Sarah smiled and whispered "The End" to a truly strange case that had luckily ended with finding real gold instead of fool's gold.

About Wendy Meadows

Wendy Meadows, a USA Today bestselling author, delights readers with her engaging stories about women sleuths. She has penned numerous books, including the beloved Sweetfern Harbor, Sweet Peach Bakery, and Alaska Cozy series. Wendy calls New Hampshire home, where she lives with her husband, two sons, two mini pigs who have big personalities, and an adorable Labradoodle who rules the roost.

Visit her website at www.wendymeadows.com for latest releases, discounts and more!

amazon.com/author/wendymeadows

bookbub.com/profile/wendy-meadows

goodreads.com/wendymeadows